CHUNKS OF TERROR
VOL. 2

By
Steve Hudgins

A QUICK WORD FROM THE AUTHOR

I'm your friendly neighborhood Maniac on the Loose. Welcome to my world. I have some terrifying things for you!

Chunks of Terror Vol. 1 has gotten lonely and needs a scary friend. And I have just the one!

Chunks of Terror Vol. 2!

It's here. 21 terrifying tales told in a "true story" style that will cover your body in goosebumps!

If you enjoy *Chunks of Terror* you'll certainly be entertained by my other Horror Anthology books, *Fragments of Fright, Blood Tingling Tales and Horror Quickies.* Direct links to all of those books can be found in the back of this book. You can also find those books and all of my others along with my audiobooks and my scary stories podcast episodes at my website: www.maniacontheloose.com

But for now, let us sink our teeth into some ghastly Chunks of Terror!

I warn you, keep your arms and legs inside the vehicle at all times and enjoy the ride!

THE POPE LICK MONSTER

The Pope Lick Monster, also known as The Goat Man, is said to be a half-man, half-goat beast that lives under a railroad trestle bridge in Central Kentucky.

The bridge itself is a sight to behold. Built in the late 1800's, the towering railroad trestle bridge is 90 feet tall and 772 feet in length.

The rusted appearance of the bridge gives the misconception that it is abandoned and no longer in use, but that's not true. The reality is that freight trains cross the Pope Lick Trestle Bridge multiple times each day.

The bridge is nestled within a scenic 4,000 acre parkland surrounded by a plush canvas of trees. There are several walking paths zigzagging throughout the parkland that offer breathtaking views of the trestle bridge, Pope Lick Creek and the neighboring woodlands.

The legend of the Pope Lick Monster goes back over 100 years when the Farnsworth Circus train derailed on the bridge. The train car housing the ensemble of the circus freak show dangled off the edge of the bridge before succumbing to gravity and crashing to the earth. All of the occupants were killed. However, they never did find the body of Grady the Goat Man.

Many believe the Goat Man to still be residing in the woods under the Pope Lick Bridge. They claim the sinister creature attempts to lure people onto the top of the bridge by using voice mimicry in hopes that the person will be hit by an oncoming train. Others suggest the Pope Lick Monster jumps from the trestle bridge onto the cars traveling down the quiet road that passes under the bridge. Some legends claim the beast attacks people with a blood stained axe.

Even if the Pope Lick Monster is nothing more than an urban legend, the fact is that more than a dozen people have died over the years when venturing onto the trestle bridge in search of the creature.

But there are many who insist that the Pope Lick Monster is indeed real, for they have encountered the beast.

The following are the tales of those who have had terrifying experiences with The Pope Lick Monster.

THE POPE LICK MONSTER
The Walking Trail

Pope Lick Road passes under the Pope Lick Bridge. On one side of the road, Pope Lick Creek passes under the bridge. And on the other side of the road, a walking trail passes under it.

I use the walking trail a few days a week for cardio. Being a single woman, I don't think it wise for me to walk down the trail by myself after dark, even though it's a nice area.

After a long day at work, I was looking forward to unwinding with a nice long walk, but I had worked late and dusk had fallen. Even so, I opted against my better judgment and took a walk on the trail after dark.

I never walk using headphones or ear buds like many people do. I like to be able to hear my surroundings. Since the walking trail winds by the edge of the woodlands, I hear the magical songs of various birds during the day. But on this night, the crickets had taken over and I was finding their constant chirp, peaceful.

Just as I was walking under the trestle bridge, I took note that the crickets had abruptly halted their chirping. It was replaced with a deafening silence. The hair stood up on the back of my neck. I could sense something was wrong.

I let out a startled squeal when I heard the heavy rustling of something near the forest's edge, just a few feet away from me. The sound was accompanied by deep, raspy breath and a cavernous guttural growl. While bears are uncommon in these parts, it wasn't impossible that's what it was.

I transitioned into a jog to get away from whatever was stirring around in the woods. Then I heard a crunching snap as it burst through the tree line. I spun around when I heard the clickety-clack of hooves on the trail behind me.

The moon was bright that night but it was behind whatever was on the trail just twenty feet away from me, thus I could only see the creature's silhouette. Whatever it was, it was huge. Seven feet tall and broad. It was evident along the silhouette's edges that the creature was covered in hair. And it seemed to be clutching something. When the creature took a step toward me, the moonlight cast a glint of light revealing that it was holding a large axe.

It was then that a car happened to be driving down Pope Lick Road toward the bridge. I immediately jumped out in front of the car, screaming for help and waving my arms around like a lunatic. As the man driving started asking me what was wrong, I turned and pointed at the monster…but it was gone and the silence of the night had been shattered by the chirps of crickets once again.

The man drove me away from there and I never walked down that trail ever again. Day or night.

THE POPE LICK MONSTER
The Bridge

It was a crisp, cool, beautiful autumn day. I had been hiking through the parkland woods. I exited the woods near the trestle bridge and was walking through a field near it, when I heard the loud scream of a young child.

It was coming from atop the bridge.

The year had been difficult on me. I was a single mother who lost my daughter to leukemia eight months previous. The scream of the child sounded just like my daughter. I didn't hesitate to spring into action.

Near the road, under the bridge is a steep slope that one can ascend to get to the top of the bridge. It has a large fence around it to make it difficult for anyone to get to the top and potentially kill themselves.

The fence didn't slow me down. I climbed over it like a squirrel and raced to the top. By the time I was able to get to the bridge, the screaming had stopped.

"Hello? Where are you?"

The voice that responded sounded exactly like my daughter's voice. The similarity was eerie.

"I'm here! Help me!"

I couldn't see anyone, but the voice was coming from the middle of the trestle bridge which was over seven hundred feet long.

"Where are you?"

"I'm stuck under the bridge! Hurry!"

I swear that voice was my daughter's. I tore down the train tracks that covered the top of the bridge as I followed the agonizing cry of the little girl who sounded like she was in pain.

When I reached the dead center of the Pope Lick Trestle Bridge, the voice went silent. I bent down onto my hands and knees and yelled out.

"Where are you?"

I got a response in the form of a cackle of laughter. But it wasn't the laughter of a little girl. It was a deep, demonic laugh.

Before I could grasp what was happening I was shocked by the reverberating, ear piercing roar of a train horn. When I looked up, I could see the train's headlight motoring toward me.

I let out a loud scream as I got up and began the race of my life against the train. I could feel the bridge shaking underneath me as the train reached the bridge. The horn continued to blare, drowning out my own screams.

I never looked back. I didn't have to. I could hear the chug of the locomotive and the metallic rattle of it gliding over the tracks. It was gaining on me. It was going to run me over and flatten me. That's what I knew in my heart, but I kept my mind positive. I kept telling myself I could do it, I could do it.

I swear I could feel the heat of the train racing up behind me as I reached the end of the bridge and jumped forward off of the tracks. The train whooshed past before I even hit the safety of the ground.

I barely survived that day. But something tried to kill me. Something mimicked the voice of my dearly departed daughter to lure me to the middle of the bridge to be ravaged by the train.

THE POPE LICK MONSTER
The Dare

Legend has it that if you walk to the middle of the Pope Lick Bridge, you could summon The Pope Lick Monster.

There were three of us. Me and my buddies, Kevin and Buzz. We were in 8th grade. During school we had been daring each other all day to go out on the bridge and call out to the Goat Man.

Honestly, I didn't think we would do it. When we started walking out to the bridge, I figured at some point we'd stop and turn around, but we didn't and suddenly there we were standing at the edge of the Pope Lick Bridge. It was so high up off the ground, it took my breath away. And the bridge was so long, we couldn't even see the other end of it. I'm not kidding.

Buzz and I were relentless in our daring of each other. It reached a point that neither of us could back down. We had to go through with it. We had to walk out on that bridge and summon the Goat Man.

At the time, we teased Kevin for not going with us, but in reality he was the smart one. He wasn't dumb enough to risk his life over some stupid dare like Buzz and I were.

As we walked down the narrow railroad bridge, it got so windy. I remember worrying that one of those wind gusts might blow us off the bridge.

Buzz was braver than I was. He kept looking down over the edge of the bridge and commenting on how far up we were and how dead we'd be if we fell. No doubt he was saying those things to scare me and make me run off the bridge to safety so he could tease me for the rest of our lives. But the fact was that he wasn't exaggerating on either point.

"Goat Man. Where are you? We summon you."

We kept calling out to the Pope Lick Monster as we walked over the bridge. And the farther we got, the more brazen Buzz became with his beckoning.

"C'mon Goat Man. Where are you? Show yourself? Where's the big bad monster at?"

It was then that we both heard the train coming. We looked at each other with fear ridden expressions. The dare was off. This was life or death and we were not reluctant to run away and get off that death trap of a bridge.

I felt the vibration of the train hitting the bridge, just before I reached Kevin and the safety of solid ground. I figured Buzz was right behind me, but that's when I heard him screaming.

"Help me! Help me!"

I turned to see Buzz standing on the bridge. He was still twenty feet away from safety as the train rushed toward him.

And he wasn't moving.

"C'mon Buzz! Run! The train is almost on you!"

"I can't! It has me! The Goat Man has me!"

Buzz kept looking down at his pant leg and his expression became even more horrified. He saw something. There was something on the side of the bridge. Something terrifying. Was it the Goat Man? Was it grabbing his pants and keeping him from escaping the train?

By the petrified look on Buzz's face, I say yes.

It was seconds later when the train crushed him. The last thing I remember seeing was Buzz's head splatter all over that bridge.

That happened over thirty years ago. To this day, I still wake up screaming from the nightmares.

THE POPE LICK MONSTER
The Road

Pope Lick Road is a quiet little two lane road. I live in the town of Fisherville. I drive under the trestle bridge every day on my way to and from work. For years I had never experienced anything unusual around the bridge, but one cold December night that all changed.

I had worked late that night and then went out to dinner and a movie with my girlfriend. By the time I dropped her off and headed home, it was well after midnight.

As I drove under the bridge, I startled when I felt a thud on the roof of my car. At first I thought someone had dropped a cinderblock down on my roof from the top of the bridge. But had that been the case, there wouldn't have still been pounding. Someone had jumped onto my roof and was hammering away at it, so I hit the brakes and came to a skidding stop. The force of my abrupt halt sent the culprit hurling off of my car and through the air. They landed in a heap about twenty feet in front of my vehicle.

I gasped as the culprit rose to their hooved feet. It was The Pope Lick Monster that I had heard about for so many years. I thought it was nothing more than a fairytale, but there it was, standing before me.

The monster was huge. Seven feet tall, maybe more. It was thick and muscular. Its legs were covered in bushy, black fur. The hair both gradually thinned out and lightened in color as it climbed up the monster's body. By the time it reached the monster's chest, the hair was snow white.

The creature had an elongated snout, piercing red eyes and long, curved horns protruding from its head. When it let forth with a deep, angry, hideous bellow, it revealed its razor teeth. And as if the monster wasn't intimidating enough, it was holding a hefty battle axe with a blood stained blade.

I wasn't going to wait around for it to make another move, so I stomped on the accelerator and took aim at the mighty beast with my car. When I was inches away from impacting the creature, it sidestepped out of the way while simultaneously bringing its axe down on the hood of the car. This caused me to spin out.

My vehicle came to a rest just off of the side of the road. The engine had died. I immediately started trying to start it back up, but the engine was just turning over and wouldn't start! I continued trying to get the engine going as I peered out my window at the enraged beast. It let out another ghastly howl of fury before charging toward me.

The creature was only a few feet from ramming my car with its horns when the engine roared to life. I floored it and spun forward back onto the road. I didn't let off the gas until I could no longer see The Pope Lick Monster in my rearview mirror.

THE BAIT

When I was 10 years old, I used to go fishing a lot with my friend Ernie. Our favorite fishing hole was Shudder Lake. It was a small lake near a forest preserve. The great thing about it was it was set deeper in the woods than most people went, so not everyone knew about it.

When we fished at Shudder Lake, we were usually the only ones there, but there was one jogger we would see occasionally. He was athletically built, had wavy brown hair and always smiled when he saw us. Sometimes he'd stop and ask us if the fish were biting. He even said he'd like to join us one day if he had time. He was always very friendly and seemed nice.

It was a Friday and Ernie and I had plans to go fishing at Shudder Lake right after school, but Ernie got sick during the day and went home early. I stopped by his house on the way home, hoping that he'd be feeling better and could still go fishing with me, but his mom said he was in bed and couldn't go out.

I thought about just going home. I usually didn't fish alone. But still, I had my pole and a carton of worms I had spent time catching during recess, so I thought I'd do a little bit of fishing by myself for an hour or two.

I hadn't been at the lake long when I started wishing I had just gone home. The fish weren't biting at all and I was getting a little bit frustrated. I was contemplating whether or not I should leave when I heard a voice.

"Hey, where's your little friend at?"

I turned to see the jogger. He was dressed in his normal jogging attire which consisted of sneakers, black spandex shorts and a colorful t-shirt. He was walking toward me.

"He's sick."

"Oh that's too bad. Are you here alone?"

I nodded, but he seemed to want further clarification.

"Your dad didn't drive you here?"

"No. I walked."

"You don't have any other friends nearby?"

I shook my head and he stepped up to me and bent down so that he was at my eye level.

"Are the fish biting today?"

"Nope. Not at all. I was just about to leave."

"What kind of bait are you using?"

I pointed to the carton of worms next to me. The jogger picked up it, removed a small, wriggling worm from the dirt within and inspected it.

"Well, no wonder you're not having any luck. The fish don't want these puny little worms. You need to get you some big, fat, juicy night crawlers!"

I nodded. He was correct. Night crawlers would have been my preference, but I couldn't find any during recess. I was about to tell him as much, but he started talking again.

"Hey, you know what kind of bait works even better than night crawlers?"

I shook my head.

"What?"

His smile widened.

"You won't believe it, but I swear it's the truth. This stuff gets the fish in a frenzy. They literally fight over it!"

I was intrigued and wanted to know more.

"Really? What is it?"

He looked around as if it were some big secret that he didn't want anyone else to know before opening his mouth like he was going to tell me, but then he paused.

"You know what? It'll be easier if I show you. I have some in my van. I'll let you have it. If it works well for you, I'll bring you more."
The jogger stood up, started walking and motioned to me.

"C'mon."

I left my fishing pole by the lake, got up and started following the man. We walked down a trail through the woods toward one of the parking lots. He chatted with me as we walked.

"So, do you have a girlfriend?"

I wrinkled up my nose in disgust.

"Girlfriend? Yuck!"

He chuckled.

"I'm with you. Girls are no fun. I like boys."

Something about that comment seemed odd. But it didn't deter me from continuing to follow him to his van. It was a beat up old white van with no windows in the back. It was the only vehicle in the parking lot. There was nobody else around. The jogger walked to the back door of the van and slid it open.

"You see that box?"

The jogger pointed to a small cardboard box that was on the other side of the van.

"The bait is inside there. Climb up in there and get it."

It was really stupid for me to do it, but I was so anxious to find out what the secret bait was that I climbed into the van and crawled toward the box. As I was doing so, the jogger said something to me that made me come to an abrupt halt.

"Do you know what sex is?"

I knew what sex was. I also knew it wasn't appropriate for him to be talking to me about it. I turned and looked at him with a confused expression. Then, out of the corner of my eye, I saw something in the jogger's van that sent a chill through my body.

Handcuffs.

At the back of the van, I noticed handcuffs that were connected to thick chains which were fastened to the wall of his darkened van.

That's when I knew I was in serious trouble. I needed to get out of that van and fast!

The jogger was blocking the exit of the door I had entered through, so I turned my attention to the door on the other side of the van. I immediately noticed that the interior handle of that door had been removed. There was no way to open it from inside.

I had no doubt that the door he was holding open had the same kind of setup. If he slid the door shut, I'd be trapped in the van, so I shot forward like a bullet and tried to squeeze past the jogger, but he began to wrestle with me.

"Oh, no you don't!"

He was trying to push me back into the van as I kicked and screamed. It was simple luck that one of my kicks hit him square in the nose and caused him to stagger backwards a few steps. That was my opportunity and I took it! I bolted from the van and began to run.

"Get back here!"

I could hear his footsteps racing up behind me as he gave chase. This guy was an athletic jogger. There was no way I could outrun him. I was doomed!

It was then that another car pulled into the parking lot. I ran screaming toward it waving my hands wildly as I cried out. The car raced up to me and stopped. I could see two people in the car, a man and woman in their early 20's. The man stopped the car and got out. I ran to him while screaming "He's chasing me!"

The young man yelled out at the jogger.

"Hey, what are you doing?"

He then called out to the girl in his car.

"Call the police!"

I was bawling at that point. As the young man held me in his arms, I turned around to see the jogger hustling to his van. He got in and burned rubber out of the parking lot.

The police arrived at the park a short bit later and I told them everything that happened.

They never caught the guy.

I try not to think about what would have happened if I hadn't escaped the van and those people hadn't arrived when they did.

I spent the rest of my childhood anxiously waiting for the day when I would be old enough that I didn't have to worry about anyone kidnapping me anymore.

DARKNESS IN THE DUNGEON

My name is Lily and I'm an avid fan of Halloween haunted attractions.

When I was a pre-teen my parents would take me to various haunted mazes and hayrides around Halloween time. These were very tame with light scares.

When I was a young teenager, I graduated to the more basic type haunted houses which entail groups of people navigating darkened halls. These attractions include creepy decorations, live actors and lots of jump scares.

Some of the more upscale haunted attractions have high production values, a lot of live actors dressed up as horrifying creatures and some very impressive animatronics.

As I got older I found the basic haunted house attractions to be lacking in intensity and I began to discover what is referred to as extreme haunts.
In case you're not familiar with what that means, think of your basic haunted house Halloween

attraction taken to the extreme! The extreme haunts are meant for adults only. They tend to be visually gory. Some of the actors are dressed in risqué costumes. And the biggest difference from the basic haunted house experience is that the actors are allowed to touch you.

There are varying degrees of extreme haunts. The more mild ones mostly involve the actors grabbing your ankles or arms as you walk through. Sometimes they grab customers and shake them or push them around in a rough manner. That's about the extent of it.

The next level of extreme haunts involves the actors grabbing customers and pulling them away from their groups and sometimes tying them to a table and administering mild electrical shocks.

And then there are the hardcore extreme haunts. These are the haunts that truly push one's physical and mental boundaries. It becomes more of an immersive experience where you become a character in your own horror movie!

I had never done a hardcore extreme haunt before, but I was very curious about the experience and felt as though I were ready to give one a try. I decided to choose one of the most intense extreme haunts in the country known as Darkness in the Dungeon

When I arrived at the Darkness in the Dungeon haunt, I immediately took heed of their immense warning sign. It stated that everyone will go through the haunt all alone. It cautioned that inside Darkness in the Dungeon one may experience touching, foul odors, fog, strobe lights, loud noises, various liquids, physical restraints, claustrophobia, abusive language, insects, suffocation, saliva and simulated rape.

I was the final customer to enter Darkness in the Dungeon that night. I stood before a large wooden door which creaked open. I was instructed to step inside. When the heavy door slammed shut behind me, I was immersed in darkness for a few seconds before a bright light zapped to life. I found myself in a white room. A woman in a nurse's outfit entered the room and presented me with a waiver to sign. It basically said they were not liable if I was injured in any way.

After signing the wavier, I was directed into a small, grimy, dimly lit room and was greeted by a man dressed in black and wearing a mask.

"What's your name?"

"Lily."

"We can touch you. You cannot touch us. Your safe word is yellow. If at any time Darkness in the Dungeon becomes too intense for you, say the safe word and your experience will immediately end. Do you understand?"

I nodded. This angered the ski masked man.

"Give me a verbal response! Do you understand?"

His tone was sharp and made me jump. I answered quickly.

"Yes. Yes, I understand."

Upon agreeing to the terms, he opened a thin door behind him which led to a long, black hallway. He shoved me into the hallway and closed the door behind me. Within seconds the lights in the hallway blacked out and I was in complete and total darkness. I literally could not see my hand in front of my face. Believe me, I tried.

I felt my way down the seemingly endless hallway. The walls were covered in cold, sticky slime of some sort. I held my hand to my nose and smelt it. The substance had a strong metallic scent. Within a few minutes I realized the hallway was growing thinner. It wasn't long before I had to turn sideways to fit down the hall. The frigid slime had coated my clothing and acted as a lubricant to help me slide through the frighteningly skinny corridor. It was a good thing that I was rather flat chested or I don't know how I would have been able to wriggle through.

Finally, the hallway began to widen, but as it got wider, the ceiling became shorter. In no time I was down on my hands and knees crawling. The farther I went, the lower the ceiling got. Eventually, I had to get flat on my chest to continue forward.

I was surprised as how well I was handling the claustrophobic experience, but realized I started patting myself on the back too soon. When I hit a dead end, a shiver of panic jolted through my body. The hallway had halted at a wall.

I was lying on my stomach with the ceiling pressing down against me. I tried to back up, but wasn't able to. I was stuck. I couldn't move. I tried to keep it together, but let forth with a scream when I suddenly heard the loud buzz of something mechanical. Being that I was in total darkness, I had no idea where the source of the grinding gears was coming from. That is until I felt the ceiling start to drop at a slow, steady pace against my back.

I was being crushed!

The ceiling was heavy. It wasn't some hollow wooden board that would give way. It felt like a giant cement block and it wasn't stopping! The weight of the ceiling was restricting my breath and I actually felt my spine pop like I was getting an adjustment from a chiropractor.

Something was wrong! The mechanism controlling the ceiling had malfunctioned and was going to crush me to death!

Knowing that I was going to die, I was just about to holler out the safe word, when I heard a deafening motorized hiss. In a flash the ceiling rose up to a normal height and a door in front of me swung open. I jumped to my feet and hurried through the door, which pounded shut behind me.

I was now in a room with rapid flashing strobe lights. It was very disorienting, but there was no mistaking the person standing in front of me who was covered in blood. It took me a few seconds to realize that the walls of the room were mirrors and that I was staring at my own reflection. The slimy substance coating the hallway was fake blood. At least I hoped it was fake.

I had only been able to focus on my reflection for mere seconds before a side door flung open and a naked man wearing a clown mask rushed into the room. He ran to me and immediately placed a clear plastic bag over my head. I stared in horror at myself in the mirror as I frantically tried to draw breath, but there was none to be had. I was being suffocated! I actually started to see black spots in my vision and I became light headed before the crazed clown pulled the bag off my head. I bent over with my hands on my thighs as I replenished my lungs with oxygen. Just as I caught my breath, the naked clown man pressed me against the mirrored wall and hissed at me.

"Do you want to use the safe word?"

I shook my head defiantly.

"No!"

"Do you want to continue?"

"Yes!"

There was something about the fact that he was asking me if I wanted to use the safe word that helped me realize this was all part of the show and no matter how bad it got, they weren't going to kill or maim me.

The naked clown man shoved me into another room which reeked of overwhelming body odor. The room was made up to be a dingy locker room. A beefy man wearing a white wife beater tank top and black pants was slicking his hair back in the mirror and turned around as though surprised by my presence. His gravelly voice echoed through the room.

"Well, well, well, what do we have here?"

He began looking me up and down in the sleaziest of ways.

"Just when I thought I couldn't get any hornier."

It was then that I remembered one of the warnings on the sign out front saying "simulated rape." This was not an experience I wanted to have! I immediately started scanning around the room for an exit. There was a door behind the man and he realized I intended to escape before he could do whatever it was he had planned.

"Oh no girly. You ain't goin' nowhere."

I tried to rush past him, but he reached out, grabbed me by my skinny arm and threw me around like a rag doll. Within seconds he had me plastered to the floor and had no problems ripping my shirt and pants off leaving me in just my bra and panties. He laid all of his weight on me as he roughly ran his hand up my thigh and stopped just inches from my crotch.

"Say the safe word."

I shook my head with defiance. This made him furious.

"Say the safe word or I'm going to bury myself inside of you!"

He couldn't rape me. I knew he couldn't. This was just an act. It was all theatrics. He might rough me up, but he wouldn't actually rape me.

"No! No, I won't say it!"

He smirked.

"Sounds to me like you want me to stick it to you. Is that what you want, bitch?"

I shook my head.

"No!"

He gripped his brawny hand around my throat, moved his face centimeters from mine and then proceeded to run his grotesque tongue up and down my cheek.

I was trying my best to be brave, but I couldn't stop the tears from rolling down my cheeks. Finally, the big man got off of me, stood up and stared down at me in disgust before spitting in my direction.

"Filthy slut. I'm afraid I might catch disease."

He pointed to the door I had tried to escape to.

"Get the hell out of here!"

He didn't have to tell me twice! I dashed out the door and into the next room.

The centerpiece of this room was a pillory. The large wooden framework was fastened to a thick post in the middle of the room. The pillory had restraining holes for head and hands. As I focused on the medieval device, someone yanked me by the back of my hair and shoved me to the pillory. In the blink of an eye they had lifted up the top half and stuck my head and hands within before dropping it shut.

I tried to lift the top board up with my wrists but it wouldn't budge. I was now a prisoner. As I awaited this next grisly experience, I realized this was more of a torture chamber than a haunt and I wasn't sure how much more I could take.

I listened to the echo of slow, steady footsteps inching toward me. Finally, the man came into view. He was tall. His tight gray t-shirt revealed his rippling muscles. He was bald headed and held a constant mischievous grin that revealed his gold front tooth.

"I like your fingers."

He ran his rough, calloused hand over my slender fingers.

"I want one of them."

The gold toothed man withdrew an unusually large pair of garden pruners and snapped them open and closed a few times before placing my pinky into the jaws. He slowly began squeezing the pruners. He was applying much more pressure than I expected and I could feel the blade beginning to pierce my skin.

"Hey!"

I was able to shift my eyes enough to see blood running down my pinky and he wasn't stopping there. How far was this psycho going to go with this? It wouldn't take much more for him to lop my finger clear off. When I shifted my eyes to his face, I could tell by his expression that he had every intention of severing my finger from my hand!

"Yellow! Yellow! Yellow!"

The man let out a deep chuckle as he continued to apply pressure to the pruners.

"Hey! I said the safe word! Now stop!"

The gold toothed man let out a laugh and I heard someone from across the room speak up.

"She said the safe word. That's enough! Stop!"

A man rushed into my view. He was wearing a navy blue jacket that appeared to have a security guard emblem on the upper arm.

The security guard stared at the gold toothed man for a long moment with a confused expression.

"Hey. You don't work here. Who the hell are you?"

The gold toothed man let out another malevolent cackle. That's when the security guard turned to me and lifted the top of the pillory up.

"Run!"

Just as I got free, the gold toothed man grabbed the security guard, slammed him against the wall and began stabbing him with the pruners.

I bolted through the door and ran through multiple rooms. As I rushed through, I noticed several of the actors in those rooms startling at my arrival as though they weren't expecting me yet. I didn't slow down to say anything to any of them. I kept running until I pushed open a door and was hit with a blast of crisp autumn air.

The ski masked man was standing outside and caught me as I rushed into his arms. The man pulled off his ski mask revealing shaggy, blonde hair.

"Congratulations, you survived Darkness in the Dungeon."

"What? I…I did it?"

"You sure did. Most people don't make it through without using the safe word."

"But…I did use the safe word. I used it when that man tried to cut off my finger."

The blonde man held the most confused expression on his face, so I held up my finger to show him the blood. He was perplexed.

"Someone tried to cut off your finger?"

I nodded.

"Yes. And then he attacked the security guard who tried to stop him!"

The blonde man's expression got serious as he looked back and forth between me and the door I exited from. He grabbed by the upper arms and shook me slightly as he spoke.

"Listen to me. Get to your car and get out of here! Hurry!"

The blonde man let me go and dashed into the building. I opted to follow the man's instructions and hurried toward my car. As I reached out for the door handle, I heard a familiar, sinister voice coming from in front of my vehicle.

"Leaving so soon?"

I gazed toward the voice and my fears were confirmed. The gold toothed man was standing in front of my car brandishing the huge pruners. His shirt was speckled with the blood of the security guard he murdered.

"I'm not done with you yet!"

I began to tremble in terror. My only chance at that point was to turn and run back to the Darkness in the Dungeon building and hope he hadn't slaughtered everyone.

As I whirled around to begin my mad dash, I froze when I saw that I had been encircled by people. I recognized some of them. The blonde man holding the ski mask, the brawny man who acted like he was going to rape me, the naked man in the clown mask and over a dozen other people. I was confused when they all began applauding. A few of them let loose with enthusiastic hooting.

Did they not see the gold toothed maniac standing behind me?

I turned to see if he was still there and he was. He too was applauding and smiling in a sincere, friendly fashion.

I spun back around when I heard the voice of the blonde haired man.

"Nobody has ever finished Darkness in the Dungeon without using the safe word. But you made it further than anyone ever has! Congratulations, Lily!"

THE CREEPY HOUSE NEXT DOOR

I'm a single father. My daughter, Ella, is 9 years old. Her mother passed away while giving birth to her. It's been just us ever since. And if I'm being honest, it has been difficult.

I'm a carpenter. I work for a home construction company. I work six days a week. My hours are long, but it's necessary to support us. The spare time I have is minimal, but I spend it all with my daughter. I'm trying. I'm trying hard. And while we're doing okay, I don't get to devote as much time to her as I would prefer.

I hire a babysitter to watch Ella from the time she gets home from school until I get home from work. I usually get home between 6pm and 9pm most days. I'm not exaggerating when I say Ella spends more time with the babysitter than with me.

We recently bought a new home. It's a two story Victorian that is much bigger than what we need, but the price was right. It needed some work, but I could do that in my spare time and it was an opportunity for me to show Ella what I do for a living. Who knows, maybe she would find it interesting.

More importantly, the house is located much closer to the majority of the jobs that I do which allows me to get home a little earlier than usual. Every extra minute I could spend with Ella is something to be treasured.

The house is situated all the way at the end of a dead end street in a very quiet suburban neighborhood. The fact that our road doesn't lead anywhere limits the street traffic to our few neighbors when they come and go.

The house next door is vacant and quite frankly, rather creepy. It too is of the Victorian style, but much larger than our house. The gloomy gray exterior is worn and neglected. Shutters hang lopsided from multiple windows, many of which are cracked. Parts of the porch are visibly rotted and sunken. It's clear that nobody has lived there in a very long time.

After a couple of months we had settled in nicely and while the extra time I had to spend with Ella was minimal, it was significant. We were both happier than we had been in some time.

It was a Thursday night when I got home very late. It was near 10:00pm and Ella was ready for bed. After I read her a bedtime story and tucked her into bed Ella said something that I wasn't expecting.

"I saw someone next door."

She motioned to the big, vacant house that loomed outside her bedroom window.

"Who did you see?"

"A man. He was standing in the window, looking at me."

I stepped to Ella's window. A window on the 2nd floor of the creepy house next door was positioned directly across from Ella's bedroom window. If a man had been standing there he would have been able to see Ella well.

I studied the darkened window and all the other windows I could see in the house. They were all dark.

"Ella, be sure to shut your curtains if you change clothes in here, do you understand?"

She smiled.

"I know, daddy."

I kissed her goodnight, went downstairs and cracked open a beer. I sat on my front porch staring at the creepy house next door for any signs of life. My fear was that vagrants may be using the house. Or drug addicts. Or high schoolers using it as a sex hangout. These were the types of people I did not want around my young daughter.

The house was even spookier at night. The moonlight cast a ghastly glow over the structure. Long shadows stretched over the house's winding porch. A layer of mist had settled along the foundation. It was the stuff of nightmares. I listened intently for any evidence of something stirring about within, but the night was deathly still and silent. And the creepy house next door appeared as vacant as ever.

My trusty babysitter was a college student named Ashley. She was in her early 20's. She loved Ella as much as Ella loved her. I called her from work the next day to tell her of Ella's experience and asked her if she would look out Ella's window from time to time to see if she noticed anyone next door.

When I arrived home, Ashley answered the door and seemed mildly flushed. I could tell something had happened.

"What's wrong? Where's Ella?"

She was quick to calm me.

"Ella is fine. Everything is all right. But just after dark, Ella was in her room and said she saw something in the window of the creepy house next door."

"What was it? What did she see?"

"She said she saw glowing eyes. I immediately went up there and looked out the window and didn't see anything unusual."

I checked on Ella. She was a little shaken, but she was a tough little girl and was handling the scare well. I asked her what she saw through the window of the creepy house next door. She echoed what Ashley had stated. Glowing eyes.

Ella isn't one to tell fables. If she said she saw something, she saw it. But it was possible that her eyes were playing tricks on her. Perhaps she saw the reflection of headlights on the glass and thought they were mischievous glowing eyes. It was also possible that one or more people were in the house next door shining flashlights around and that's what she saw.

I decided to take a closer look and walked over to the creepy house next door. It was a foreboding structure. I felt goosebumps break out on my arms as I approached it. I followed the cobblestone walkway that was overtaken by weeds. It led to the rickety porch. It creaked with anger as I put my weight on it and stepped up to the front door. The door was thick, dark stained wood with a rusted Egyptian faced doorknocker.

I stood at the door for a few minutes and listened. The air was still. The surrounding nightlife was silent. If someone were in that house scurrying about, I figured I'd hear them and my assumption was quickly proven correct.

I heard the loud creak of a door within the house open.

Someone was in there, so I put the door knocker to use and rapped it against the door.

All was silent for a moment and then I heard a door slam shut.

I knocked again, this time using my knuckles.

"Hello? Is anyone in there?"

Nothing. No response. No sound. Just quiet.

I carefully stepped up to one of the front porch windows, cupped my hand against the glass and looked in, but it was pitch black inside. There was no illumination whatsoever. After a few more minutes, I gave up and went back home.

The following day something rare occurred. I got off work early and made it home just after Ella arrived home from school. I let Ashley go home and Ella and I got to work on some home improvements. We spent the majority of the afternoon replacing the lattice around our front porch. Ella either enjoyed carpentry or was simply happy that I was home early because she was beaming the entire time.

After we ate dinner, I did the dishes and Ella went to her bedroom to change into her night clothes. I startled when I heard her scream. I raced up the stairs. When I barged into Ella's room, I found her staring out her bedroom window. She was white as a ghost and was trembling with fear.

"What happened, Ella?"

She pointed at the window of the creepy house next door.

"I saw the man again."

I quickly looked outside but didn't see anyone.

"Was he watching you?"

Ella shook her head.

"He moved past the window, but he wasn't walking."

I was confused.

"What do you mean?"

"It was like…he was floating. I think he's a ghost, daddy! I think the creepy house next door is haunted!"

I hugged my daughter tightly and assured her everything would be okay. I tried to divert her attention by promising her that I'd make us some popcorn and that we'd watch a funny movie before bed. That seemed to temporarily get her mind off of the apparition she was positive she saw.

As Ella hurried downstairs to get the popcorn making necessities in order, I took another long hard gaze out her window at the creepy house next door in hopes of seeing something and to my surprise I did!

It was a man. Medium build. Late 30's. He was a very well kempt, dapper gentleman in a custom fitted three piece suit with matching tie and hat. He exited the house next door and disappeared into the darkness.

This is not the type of person I was expecting to find exiting the house. I expected a vagrant drifter or the junkie type. The man I saw didn't fit that profile.

Who was he? That was a question I intended to get an answer to.

The next night, I arrived home just before dusk. I went straight to the creepy house next door to pay my apparent neighbor a visit. I wanted to find out who he was and verify that he belonged there.

When I gave the door a hefty bang with the door knocker, the large, heavy door swung open. Obviously the door had a bad latch to go along with the rest of its deterioration.

I stuck my head into the house and was met with the scent of mildew and the distant stale stench of rotting meat.

"Hello? Anyone home?"

The place was in shambles. There was no furniture. There were multiple holes in several sections of the floor. Everything I could see was draped in dust and cobwebs. There was no way anybody could live there.

"Hello?"

Nobody was answering me and since the door had opened on its own, I decided to accept that as an invitation to wander through the house. One of the first things that stood out was a winding staircase that led to the 2nd floor. The bannister was thick and appeared hand carved. The steps were incredibly heavy under my feet. So much so that I bent down and wiped the dust away to see what they were made of.

Marble.

This was quite the fancy house at one time. I was curious as to how it had fallen into such disrepair.

I ventured upstairs and found my way into the empty bedroom that was across from Ella's room. It was a large room. The vintage flowered wallpaper had yellowed with time. The dusty floor showed no evidence of footsteps or any other sign of someone having been there recently. But I knew Ella saw something and I was determined to find out what.

I moved back down to the main floor. I began following the decaying aroma and as I moved closer to the source, I realized that it was the stink of death. Likely an animal had come to the house to die. Feeling adventurous, I followed the disgusting scent to a door in the main hallway.

As I opened the door, I was bowled over by the reek of decomposition. I covered my mouth and let out a few hefty coughs before I noticed a flight of unsteady wooden stairs that descended down into darkness.

Whatever had died was in the pitch black basement. And I had come this far so I was going to follow my nose.

I pulled out a small penlight from my pocket which illuminated the unsteady stairs enough to navigate them. I was thankful that the handrail was sturdy and able to hold the majority of my weight. One thing was certain, there was no way I was going to get out of that basement fast!

When I reached the concrete floor of the basement, I felt the stirring of water under my feet. It appeared to be an inch deep. It wasn't a surprise that the basement was holding water. Why should it be any different than the rest of the decrepit house?

I sloshed my way through the shallow, stagnant water deeper into the cavernous basement. The disgusting rotten smell was beginning to overwhelm me. I could actually taste it in my mouth which caused me to gag. When I felt bile rising up my esophagus I officially decided to throw in the towel and head back upstairs.

As I wheeled around, the beam of my pen light flashed against the source of the stink. I was face to face with the skeletal remains of a person. Hunks of dried, rancid flesh hung from the bones. The sight was sickening and I instinctively rushed backwards and bumped into something that felt…bony.

I quickly whirled around and focused my beam on the second decaying body. As I moved my beam around the moldy basement, I discovered the remains of another body. And another. And another. Some were fresher than others, but they were all in various stages of decay.

I was panicked and frantic as I spun around the basement trying to maneuver myself around the maze of corpses back to the basement stairs, but I found myself frozen in terror and confusion when the beam of my penlight halted on a coffin.

The coffin was exquisite. It was constructed of African Blackwood. It was visually breathtaking. Intricate hand carvings covered the base. Its beauty was out of touch with the rest of the filthy, crumbling house.

When the coffin lid opened by itself, I jumped backwards, stumbled and fell to the dank floor. Even upon falling, I kept the beam of light trained on the mysterious coffin and watched as the dapper gentleman sprang upright from the casket like a stiff mechanical board.

When he turned his head, affixed his black eyes on me and smirked, I wanted to run, but I couldn't move. I wasn't sure if that was due to fear or some kind of hypnotic hold the man had on me, but I was motionless as the man glided toward me, never touching the floor beneath him.

If this…thing, was going to kill me, I'd man up and accept my fate, but Ella needed me. Her mother was gone. All she had was me. And thus I found myself begging for my life.

"Please, don't kill me. I have a daughter."

The man's voice was smooth as silk.

"Yes, I've seen her. And she has seen me. That is most unfortunate."

Was that some kind of veiled threat on my daughter's life? She had seen him and now she had to die? My fear turned to anger.

"If you lay one hand on her I'll rip you to pieces!"

The man found my threat amusing and let out a short chuckle before speaking up.

"What do you do for a living, fine sir?"

"What?"

"How I despise repeating myself, so don't ask me to do so again. Now, if you want your daughter to live, please answer my question."

I quickly answered.

"I'm a carpenter."

He nodded.

"Ah yes. I heard your hammering yesterday. Tell me, if you had unlimited funds, do you believe you could restore this home to its former glory?"

I crinkled my brow in thought. Did he say unlimited funds? I almost asked for clarification but he had made it clear that he didn't like repeating himself so I assumed that was accurate.

"Yes. With unlimited funds, I could do anything you wanted with this house."

The man gave a nod, clasped his hands behind his back and began floating around the basement effortlessly as he spoke.

"As you may have ascertained by now, I am what one may refer to as a vampire. Please forgive the dreadful appearance of my dwelling for I have been without a caretaker for decades and I'm not very handy, myself."

Vampire. That's what he said. I hadn't misunderstood him. The word echoed through my mind as the creature of the night continued.

"You'll be my caretaker. You'll restore my humble abode. You'll clean up after me."

The vampire motioned to the array of dead bodies in the basement.

"You'll stay here during the day to make sure nobody disturbs my slumber. And you'll do anything else I require. In exchange, I'll give you a stipend five times what you currently earn. And the assurance that nothing will *ever* harm your daughter."

The vampire stared at me with glowing eyes. His offer seemed more like a demand, but the benefits were not lost on me. I would never have to be apart from Ella ever again. And she'd always be safe. What more could I ask for?

I looked up at the vampire. It was clear he was growing impatient with my lack of immediate response.

"We have a deal, yes?"

I stood up and brushed myself off before giving my answer. My life…Ella's life would change forever if I accepted. How I hoped it would be for the better.

"Yes. We do."

THE DISEASE AND THE CURE

I'm a lead scientist for a biological warfare division of the defense department.

We've created many infectious agents over the decades which would be quite deadly to most of the Earth's inhabitants if ever released. If I ever told you how many such maladies we possess, you wouldn't sleep at night.

However, none of them compare to the deadly disease we recently generated. It hasn't been given a formal name as of yet. Currently we refer to it as T-1000.

T-1000 comes in the form of a clear liquid that is contained in a tiny glass bottle. We have produced cases of the disease even though I explained that it's so potent, we really only need one.

If the liquid were poured out of the bottle the contents would turn to vapor before it hit the ground. It instantly reproduces at an alarming rate when introduced to oxygen. Once airborne, the entire planet would be infected in less than one full day.

Once ingested via breath, the subject's internal organs instantly liquefy and death will occur within seconds. I've been able to reduce the potency to the point that it is only effective on the human species.

How will this devious disease be used? That's for some military commander or politician to decide. I just make the stuff.

Having such a deadly disease won't be much use to anyone without the cure of which I recently succeeded in creating. It too is a clear liquid housed in a small bottle. Once the liquid is consumed the subject has lifelong immunity to the T-1000 disease.

In my hand, I hold the one and only bottle of the antidote. Mass production is scheduled to begin today, though I don't have the energy to proceed.

I didn't sleep last night, you see.

This was not due to anything related to my profession. This was due to an occurrence within my home life.

My wife is the definition of beauty. Physical perfection. Intelligence that surpasses mine. My heart is hers. I am nothing without her. I'd literally go mad without her by my side.

Last night my wife told me she was leaving me for the military commander who is in charge of my division. She claims to want someone who holds more control than a lowly scientist.

If only she knew the power I currently wielded. In one hand I hold the power to kill everyone on the planet. In the other, I hold the power to save them.

My wife would argue that I only create such things. I don't have the power to use them.

My world is shattered. Much like the bottle that once held the T-1000 disease.

The disease is now airborne, but not to worry. I drank down the one and only bottle that contained the cure. I'll be fine.

Sorry I can't say the same about my wife, her lover and…well…the rest of you.

THE PHANTOM OF THE SEMINARY
Bobby

We were the class of 87. When we graduated high school, I stayed home and enrolled at a local community college while the majority of my good friends went away to major universities.

My closest friends stayed within reasonable driving distance from our town and we all decided to make a pact. We would stay in regular contact with each other and wouldn't allow for the gradual drifting apart process that tended to occur with most high school friendships.

For the most part, I had done well with staying in touch with the gang. I called them all weekly, would write them letters and most weekends I would drive out to one of their colleges to spend some quality time with them.

The one friend I had neglected was named Dan. He was the one who opted for a school that was a five hour drive away. I had yet to visit him and hadn't even spoken to him in over a month.

Dan was the sophisticated member of our circle. He read books while the rest of us were yucking it up, watching mindless action movies. He appreciated a fine scotch while we specialized in cheap beer. He took in the enchanting sounds of classical music while the rest of us numbskulls head banged to heavy metal.

It wasn't a surprise to any of us when Dan chose a much different career path than the rest of us. He was studying to be a priest at a private catholic college.

It was good to hear Dan's voice when he called me. We chatted for a few minutes before he mentioned in passing that none of us had made the trip out to see him yet. He wasn't complaining, but I could tell from the tone of his voice that it bothered him. I felt bad, so when he mentioned that most of the other students living at the seminary would be gone the upcoming weekend and that he'd practically have the entire building to himself, I made a commitment to finally take the trip to see him.

It was really nice to see Dan. He didn't look great though. He was pale and his face was drawn as though he had lost weight. Still he was anxious to show me around and I thoroughly enjoyed the tour he gave me of the historic college grounds. It was a small, charming campus that was enjoying peak fall colors.

After the tour Dan took me to his favorite restaurant, a small bistro a few blocks from campus that had wonderful, fresh food. I of course had a few beers with dinner, while Dan, not surprisingly, enjoyed an array of scotch varieties. By the time we got back to the seminary, we were both on the drunken side.

The seminary itself was the oldest building on campus. It was a long, four story brick structure with impressive columns near the entrance. Dan explained that the building opened as a hotel in the mid 1800's and was used as a hospital during the Civil War. For a brief time after that it was used as an asylum before the college purchased the building and turned it into the seminary it still is today.

Dan's small, private dorm room was on the 2nd floor. He told me I was free to stay in any vacant room throughout the seminary. Dan wasn't exaggerating when he said he practically had the entire building to himself that weekend. I literally only saw two other people walking down his hall the entire time I was there. He mentioned to me that if I wanted privacy, that nobody was currently occupying any of the rooms on the 4th floor. He then went on to tell me that some claimed that floor was haunted.

"Haunted?"

That immediately piqued my curiosity. He knew it would. All of my friends were well aware that I was a big fan of ghost stories, haunted house movies and that I would occasionally partake in a paranormal investigation if the opportunity arose.

We continued to drink the night away as I peppered him with questions about the haunted history of the building. Dan said that he didn't have any personal experiences but that some of the students residing in the seminary claimed to have seen shadowy figures moving throughout the halls. Others said they heard voices when they knew nobody else was around and one friend of his insisted that every so often someone would knock on his door in the middle of the night, but when he'd get up to answer it, nobody would be there.

"They say there's a phantom that lives in room 44. It's supposed to be the most haunted room in the entire building."

The second Dan muttered those words, I knew where I was going to be sleeping that night! I was always up for a chance to have a ghostly encounter!

It must have been after 3:00am when Dan passed out in mid-sentence and I staggered my way up to the 4th floor and entered room 44. The room smelled musty and was quite chilly. Clearly it hadn't been used by anyone in some time, but I was drunk off my ass. I didn't care. As long as it had somewhere soft for me to lay my head, I was set.

The room was dark. There was probably a light switch around that I could turn on if I wanted, but I was seconds away from passing out, so I didn't bother looking. I set my focus on the outline of the bed I could make out in the corner of the room. I collapsed onto the bed and pulled the covers over me.

As I quickly began to drift off, I was disturbed by a sound coming from across the room. It was a rhythmic, raspy sound.

It was the sound of someone breathing.

I opened my eyes and looked up. The only illumination in the room was coming from a streetlight outside the window and it was minimal at best. I couldn't see much, but thought I saw a silhouette of a person standing against the far wall.

"Hello?"

The word was barely out of my mouth when the blankets were ripped off my body by an unseen force. If I weren't in such an inebriated state, I may have tried to communicate with whatever was sharing the room with me. Instead, I panicked and rushed to the door only to find it locked. I tried turning the knob but it would not move. I attempted to pull the door open by force, but it wouldn't budge. I could feel cold breath on the back of my neck when I heard the hissing words.

"You're mine!"

I spun around and ran to the window which faced the main dormitory across the way. I tried to open the window, but it felt like it was nailed shut. The campus was quiet and lonely, but I did see one person meandering toward the main dorm entrance, so I began pounding relentlessly on the window as I screamed for help. He must have heard me as he turned and gazed up my way. I could clearly see an expression of horror overtake his face. It took me a few seconds to realize he wasn't looking at me. His stare was affixed on something next to me. I turned my head to see what it was…and screamed.

THE PHANTOM OF THE SEMINARY
Drake

I partied at a bar until it closed down at 2:00am. Then I talked my way into a frat party and hung out there for another hour or so. I was listening to some tunes on my headphones as I wandered through the campus toward my dorm.

Once I reached the front of the dorm, I removed my headphones and the funky music was replaced by heavy pounding and muffled cries of panic. I turned around and instantly saw the young man pounding on one of the 4th floor seminary windows.

I knew one of the seminary students. His name was Dan. He was a nice fella who loved a good scotch. I remember him telling me once that there was a phantom that haunted one of the rooms of the 4th floor. At first I thought the young man I saw banging on the window was the phantom in question, but his horror riddled face said otherwise.

That's when I saw it. The phantom of the seminary.

It was in the same room as the young man and was standing in front of the next window over. The phantom was tall and lean. It looked like a floating black hooded cloak. It was difficult to make out much detail until it looked out the window directly at me.

I could feel my face shrivel up in terror. The face with the cloak looked like a cloud of white smoke with evil slanted eyes. I saw no other features until a twisted, maniacal black mouth suddenly materialized. It only held its sinister gaze on me for a moment before it turned back to the panicked young man and charged.

For a brief moment, the young man was shrouded in a black mist and then instantly the mist dissipated inward and the young man dropped out of sight.

I called the cops. Of course I couldn't tell them what I saw. I was drunk and the story was too fantastic. So I just said I saw someone throwing a fit on the 4th floor of the seminary and that it looked like they needed help.

The next morning when I looked out my dorm room window, I saw an ambulance outside the seminary. I rushed outside and found out that the young man I had seen the previous night had died. Apparently there was no sign of foul play. The medical report ruled the cause of death, cardiac shock caused by a massive surge of adrenaline.

I remember that one of the emergency medical technicians looked particularly distraught after exiting the seminary. I approached him and asked him what was wrong. He was still visibly shaken when he told me what he saw. The deceased young man's face was frozen in a state of perpetual fear.

He was literally scared to death.

THE PHANTOM OF THE SEMINARY
Dan

I was considered the eccentric member of our friend group. I was liked, but different. When I opted to travel much farther away for school than anyone else, I expected a gradual drop off in communication that may gradually result in my close friends eventually becoming casual friends. What I didn't expect was to be completely forgotten almost immediately.

At first I got a few letters and an occasional call. After a month those things became rarities. At first I was disappointed. Then I became irritated. Eventually, I was angered by the situation. I felt as though I had been deserted by the group.

I tried my best to focus on my new school life and to settle into my new seminary surroundings. When I arrived at the seminary I was told by the seminary rector that I could have my pick of rooms on the 4th floor. He recommended room 44 as being the best room in the entire seminary, so I snagged it.

My first night in the room was troubling. I woke up in the middle of the night to the sound of heavy breathing coming from across the room. I jumped out of bed and turned on the light. There was nobody there.

The following night, I was awakened by hot breath against the back of my neck. I reached over and could feel a boney body lying in the bed next to me. I jumped out of bed in a panic and turned on the light, but there was nobody there.

It was my third night in room 44 when I had a nightmare. I was tied down on my bed and couldn't move. I could hear deep, ghastly laughter as someone…or something ran their long, sharp finger nails down my back. When I woke up, my back was burning. I hurried to the bathroom, lifted up my shirt and found three distinct scratches on my back.

I wasn't sure what was happening to me. Was I having some kind of mental breakdown? Was it possible that all of my experiences were in my head? Regardless, I moved out of room 44 the following day and chose a room on the more populated 2nd floor.

Everything was fine after that for the next week until I woke up one night to a hissing voice in my ear.

"You're mine!"

Nobody was in my room. Believe me, I checked thoroughly. How I hoped it was all some kind of practical joke, but I found out the next day it wasn't.

I was combing my hair in the mirror when I realized I wasn't looking at myself, but rather a foggy image of a cloaked face with thin, black eyes and a ghastly, mangled mouth. It let forth with the most hideous screech and the mirror shattered.

I wasn't crazy! This was really happening!

At the risk of being considered a lunatic, I decided to speak to the seminary rector about my experiences. I'll always remember the guilty expression he held coupled with sad, teary eyes.

"I'm so sorry, Dan. What have I done?"

The rector collapsed into his office chair and with trembling hands poured himself a drink.

"You're cursed, aren't you?"

He knew! He knew what I was going through!

"Yes! What's happening to me? What is this?"

He wolfed down his drink before explaining.

"The phantom of the seminary. It lurks through the halls of the 4th floor and resides within room 44. I've lived with it for decades, but I couldn't do it any longer! God forgive me!"

"What are you talking about?"

"The phantom! It's attached itself to you. Much like it did to me over thirty years ago. I don't know what it is or where it came from. I just know that it's evil. I tried to shoulder the burden so that nobody else would ever have to experience it, but I couldn't do it any longer. Its constant malevolent presence had worn me down. It was sucking the life out of me."

"What did you do?"

The rector broke down for a moment before regaining his composure by taking in several deep breaths.

"It's that room. Room 44. For the past three decades, I kept it locked tight. I was the only one to go inside. It attaches itself to whoever enters. For over thirty years I carried it with me so nobody else would suffer…but I couldn't any longer…after decades of constant torment, I broke down. You showed up at my weakest moment and I encouraged you to take room 44. God forgive me, I'm sorry."

I left the rector sobbing in his office. As enraged as I was by him inflicting the evil burden upon me, I was thankful that I knew how to rid myself of it. The only question was who would my victim be?

Being new in town, I hadn't any enemies, so who better to choose than one of the friends who I felt had abandoned me. Bobby had a fascination with the paranormal. I would have no problem getting him to enter room 44. I laid a subtle guilt trip on him to get him to visit and the rest is history.

I didn't mean to kill him. I just wanted to rid myself of the phantom.

If there's a bright side to the story it's that several people have been inside room 44 since that day with no haunting effects. I believe when the phantom attached itself to Bobby and Bobby died, the phantom died with him.

YOU'RE GOING TO DIE TONIGHT

It was Friday night. It had been a long week at work and I was looking forward to having a girl's night at home with my roommate Crystal and my best friend, Maria.

When I got home from work I found Crystal to be sick as a dog. She was lying on the couch, covered in a blanket and dripping with sweat. I hurried to her and felt her forehead with the back of my hand. She was burning up with fever.

"Crystal, you're really sick. Do you want me to take you to the emergency room?"

Crystal lethargically opened her eyes which had a glassy appearance to them. She seemed to be having a difficult time deciphering who I was as she struggled to spit out some words.

"Rose? Rose…is that you?"

"Yes, it's me. I think I should take you to the hospital. You're burning up!"

She slowly shook her head.

"No."

Crystal happened to be a nurse. So I asked her if perhaps I could call up one of her doctor friends and have them stop by to look at her. Again, she declined.

"It's not necessary. My fever will break in a few hours and I'll be fine."

After releasing those words, she closed her eyes and fell into a deep sleep.

So much for our girl's night plans. But Maria was still coming over. When she arrived, I'd suggest we salvage the night by us two going out for a bite to eat and then maybe some drinks. It was then that the phone rang. Just before I answered it, Crystal's eyes popped open and she stared at me with a hauntingly serious expression.

"It's Maria. She's…she's going to…cancel."

After struggling to get the words out, Crystal laid her head back down and dozed off.

I answered the phone and it was indeed Maria. And she was cancelling. She said a guy she liked at work asked her out on a date and she didn't want to pass up the opportunity. I understood.

"It looks like it's just me."

As disappointed I was that our plans for the night had fallen through, a quiet night at home sounded appealing. I'd order a pizza, watch some TV, take a hot bath and relax.

After ordering a large pizza with mushrooms and onions, I sat down in my favorite recliner and fumbled for the television remote controller. As I did so, Crystal opened her eyes again. She was looking directly at me, but her eyes seemed unfocused as though she were looking past me at something else. She seemed dazed and confused, but spoke deliberately.

"You can't watch TV. The cable is going to go out."

After her bold statement Crystal fell back to sleep. I stared at the wall as I thought for a moment. She was correct about Maria cancelling, could she be right about this too?

I turned the TV on and it was fine. The show I wanted to watch was playing and there were no issues. At least not until ten minutes later, when the cable went out. The screen started flashing and then a still image appeared which read: Technical Issues. Please Stand by.

At first I was frustrated that the cable was out. Then it dawned on me that Crystal was right. Again.

But how?

How did she know that Maria was going to cancel? How did she know the cable would go out?

What was going on?

It was then that I heard a knock at the door. It was my pizza, no doubt. As I got up and started toward the door, I halted when I heard Crystal's wheezing voice calling to me.

"Rose…Rose. Your pizza order. It's…it's…"

I looked back at her as her voice trailed off. Her eyelids were half closed and I could see her struggling not to drift off. She managed to articulate her final word before nodding off again.

"…wrong."

I pondered what she said for a few seconds. My pizza order was wrong. If she were correct on this one, I was going to freak out.

I hurried to the door. The pizza deliveryman stood there holding my pizza and a large smile. I instantly opened the top of the pizza box as he held it. I stared at the toppings of the pizza in shock. The deliveryman recognized this and spoke up.

"Ma'am, is everything okay?"

I shook my head and spoke in a slow, stunned voice.

"This is supposed to be mushrooms and onions. But it's mushrooms and black olives."

The deliveryman looked at the pizza and then referred to the ticket.

"Oh, I'm so sorry about this. Looks like they screwed up the order. I can either place a new order or I can just let you have this one at half off."

I was in a bit of a stupor as I accepted his half price offer and paid him.

Crystal was right again. Somehow in her fever-ridden state she was having premonitions that were coming true!

I set the pizza down on the counter, rushed over to Crystal and began shaking her gently in an attempt to wake her up. I had to find out what other premonitions she might be having!

I wasn't shaking her more than a few seconds when her eyes shot open, wide with fear. She latched on to my shirt and pulled me close. Her voice was weak and her words were mumbled.

"You're going to…die…tonight!"

With that, she closed her eyes and collapsed onto the couch.

Her words were disjointed and muttered. I wanted to make sure I understood her correctly. I thought maybe there were a couple words in there that I didn't hear right. At least, I hoped so! I shook her vigorously in an attempt to wake her from her slumber, but it was no use. She was out like a light.

I was going to die tonight?

That's what she said. It was garbled, but clear enough. And she was correct about her other premonitions, why wouldn't she be right about this one too?

What was I supposed to do now? How was I going to die? And could I prevent it?

I had to wait for Crystal to wake up again to get the answers to my questions. In the meantime, I'd have a nice slice of pizza…

No! What if that's how I died? What if I choked to death on a piece of pizza?

I shoved the pizza box away and felt paranoia wash over me. I had planned on taking a hot bath, but I couldn't do that now. The bathtub was upstairs. I might fall down the stairs and break my neck! Or I may pass out in the bathtub and drown!

A knock on the door made me gasp.

It was a heavy knock. And it was relentless. The person wouldn't stop knocking. They were practically banging on the door! Could it be a mad man? A crazed serial killer? Is that how I was going to die? Was I going to be murdered by this maniac?

When I heard the doorknob begin to jiggle, I grabbed my handgun. I was not going to let this psycho kill me!

I stepped closer to the door, steadied myself by taking in a few deep breaths, aimed my gun and prepared to fire. I watched as the doorknob turned and the door swung open. I placed my finger on the trigger and began to squeeze…

"Rose! No!"

I quickly removed my nervous finger from the trigger.

"Maria? What are you doing here? I almost shot you!"

"I knocked but there wasn't an answer, so I used the key under the mat. I didn't think you would mind...I certainly didn't think you'd kill me over it!

It took us both a few moments to regain our composure. Finally, Maria explained.

"That guy I had a date with. He had to cancel at the last minute, so I thought I'd come over and surprise you!"

I noticed that Maria was holding a box in her hands. Before I could ask what it was, Crystal startled us both when she jumped from bed, stared at me and screamed.

"You're going to dye...your hair...tonight."

With that she passed out once again. And I buckled over in relief.

It wasn't the word "die" as in dead, I heard her mutter. It was "dye" as in color. The "your hair" part was what was so garbled that I couldn't understand it.

I looked down at the box Maria was holding. It was blond hair dye. And Crystal was correct again. Maria helped me dye my hair that night.

A few hours later Crystal's fever broke and she felt fine. I told her about everything she said, but she had no memory of any of it and never had another premonition again.

HUNTED

When I say I'm a king among men, I don't say that arrogantly. I say that because it's a fact.

I live in a little steel mill town in Northern Pennsylvania. Most of the townsfolk look up to me. Some practically worship me. I should have left when I graduated high school. I might have been able to get away without causing too much disorder back then. Instead I made the mistake of going to work in the steel mills and further entrenching myself within the town.

Now I'm stuck here, like a rusted anchor imbedded in the darkest depths of the ocean floor.

I do believe I'm going crazy.

With each passing year, my desire to break free from the town's hold grows stronger, but such an escape would not be possible without significant collateral damage.

My four closest friends, Spike, Stan, John and Nick whom I affectionately refer to as "the boys" all depend on me. They need my approval before they make any decisions. Buying a car, a boat, a house, they won't do it without me giving them the okay. Hell, they refuse to pull the trigger on a date unless I tell them the woman in question meets with my satisfaction.

If I were to leave now they'd be lost. I remember the day I floated the idea of me fleeing the town…and them. They were devastated. Spike had a panic attack on the spot. That's when I knew I could never leave them alone.

Most people might assume that if I left, the others would adapt. And sure, there might be some truth to that. I expect they would continue on, but they'd be virtual zombies, lethargically plodding their way through their meaningless lives.

I could never resign them to such a state. It would be nothing short of cruelty to do so. So I stay. And with each passing year I feel my sanity abandon me that much more.

The one outlet in my simple life is deer hunting. I live for that two week getaway in the mountains every November. Of course, the boys always go with me. I don't think they could be without me that long.

While I may go to the mountains with the boys and we all share a cabin, when it comes to the actual act of hunting, I've always explained to them that I hunt alone.

It's those few hours each day during that fleeting two week period each year when I feel alive. The fresh air fills my lungs. An unbearable weight is lifted from my shoulders. I break the chains that bind me to that little town. I'm free from that anchor that keeps me there.

It was the final day of our latest trip and I didn't even bother to take my gun into the wilderness with me. I simply found a stump and sat there, breathing in my freedom.

I heard the gun shots. Four of them in rapid succession. Being that it was hunting season I didn't think anything of it until I went back to the cabin that night. Spike, Stan, John and Nick had all been shot directly between the eyes. Their deaths were quick, no doubt. I'm happy about that.

I never went back to the little steel town after that day. I went directly to my new life in the bluegrass region of Kentucky. I have a cabin in the rolling hills and live off of the land. The white tail deer are abundant and there's never a shortage of food.

I've been quite effective at distancing myself from that fateful day when my closest friends were shot to death. I was in the mountains enjoying the peaceful nature when it happened. With each passing day, I believe that scenario a little bit more. Perhaps at some point, it will be reality in my own mind.

I don't know if anyone will ever truly put it together that I was the one that killed the boys. But even if they do, they'll never find me.

I'm free.

THE CREATURE FROM THE BLACK FOREST

My name is Joe Sharp. I'm a private detective.

I'm the guy who gets called when nobody else can get the job done. I'm not cheap but I'm worth every penny. For the most part.

I was hired by a woman named Simona Kerber to find her missing fiancé, Rhett Dashwood. Evidently Mr. Dashwood had retired to his private screening room to watch an obscure film he recently acquired.

According to Miss Kerber, when she checked on him hours later, there was no sign of him. After a substantial amount of time went by, she alerted the authorities and they did an investigation. The cops not only found no signs of foul play, they didn't find any evidence at all. The case is still open, but Miss Kerber said the police have implied that they simply think Mr. Dashwood walked out on her. Hell, it wouldn't have been the first time a prospective husband had second thoughts and made a fast getaway.

Miss Kerber insists they were an extremely happy and compatible couple. On top of that, Mr. Dashwood was over the moon with his newly acquired rare film and was looking forward to throwing some kind of fancy shmancy screening for a bunch of big wigs who were willing to pay top dollar to view the obscure film.

That made sense to me. Even if this guy was looking to back out of the marriage, he certainly wouldn't walk out on all the loot he was about to haul in from that private screening.

As I gathered more information from Miss Kerber about the film in question, things got intriguing fast.

Miss Kerber led me into Mr. Dashwood's private screening room. It looked like a mini-movie theater with a dozen plush, crimson theater seats positioned in front of a large screen.

At the front of the theater was an old, metal film canister.

The canister showed its age. It was a distressed shade of pale gray and was riddled with small dents and splotches of rust. A crude hunk of silver duct tape had been slapped on the side of the canister. The name of the movie was written on it in sloppy handwriting.

The Creature from the Black Forest.
Run Time: 83 minutes

Miss Kerber didn't share her fiancé's passion for film, thus she wasn't able to divulge as much information as I would prefer, but what she had was good enough for a jumping off point. She said the movie was one of the rarest on the planet and was coveted by serious collectors the world over. Her fiancé had explained to her that one of the reasons the film was in such demand was because of the rumor that it was cursed.

I had a strong urge to watch the film. Perhaps I would find a clue buried within the frames of the movie. But ultimately, I decided it would be wise to find out more about what exactly I had my hands on before making a reckless decision.

My first stop was to a local sex fetish joint known as Club Fun. It was a real freak show, let me tell ya', but I knew a guy named Harvey Lamar that hung out there. He was well attuned when it came to old films. I wanted to pick his brain and see if he knew anything about this supposed cursed film.

When I stepped into the darkened foyer of Club Fun the heavy beating bass of the club's music reverberated through my body. I heard a deep, breathy male voice emerge from one of the gloomy corners.

"Are you a virgin?"

That was this pervert's way of asking me if it was my first time at Club Fun.

"Piss off, freak."

I pushed my way past the foyer's curtain and began walking down the dimly lit corridor. It wasn't my first time at Club Fun. Unfortunately for me, a lot of people with valuable information frequented the sex club. Believe me, I always gave my hands a dousing of extra strength sanitizer upon leaving that joint.

As I walked down the first hallway, a fully naked woman walked my way. She clearly wasn't fond of body grooming, if you know what I mean. As I turned down an adjoining corridor I was greeted by a shapely woman dressed as Little Po Peep. She was spanking a man dressed as a sheep with a cane. I hurried past them and recognized a familiar face.

Platinum.

Platinum was a sleazy hooker in a platinum wig, fishnet stockings and a tight tank top that accentuated her ample rack. She was a walking dictionary of Club Fun clientele.

"Joe Sharp. What brings you to my neck of the woods?"

The prostitute strutted to me and ran her finger down my chest as she looked me up and down. I held a ten dollar bill up in front of her face.

"Do you know a guy named Harvey Lamar? I know he hangs out here somewhere."

Platinum quickly snatched the cash from my hand.

"Harvey likes to play backgammon while people have sex in the same room. Turn left at the end of the corridor. Find the room that has the word nasty scribbled on it. But don't go in there! The room you'll find Harvey in is two doors past it on the left."

I gave Platinum a nod.

"Thanks."

"Anytime. And if you're in the mood for a little extracurricular activity later, I'll give you a discount."

I rolled my eyes as I hurried down the corridor, turned left and found the "nasty" room. Beyond the door I could hear someone screaming out in pain whilst being applauded by a large group of people. I didn't even want to know what was going on in there. I followed Platinum's instructions, walked two doors down, gave the unassuming plain metal door a knock and entered.

There was Harvey Lamar. He was out of place in his business casual attire and neatly trimmed beard. He was sitting at a table in the front of the room with a backgammon board in front of him. Sitting across from him was an attractive woman dressed as though she just got off work from an office job. They were nursing fine wine and pleasant piano music was playing over the room's speakers.

In the back of the room a naked guy in a hockey mask was positioned behind a red headed woman wearing a clown nose. He was pounding away at her like a jack hammer while she hollered out in ecstasy. Her shameless moans of pleasure were so damned loud I had to raise my voice to be heard over her.

"Hey Harvey, you ever hear of a rare film called The Creature from the Black Forest?"

Harvey did not make eye contact with me and continued to play backgammon while he spoke.

"Ah yes. Rare film indeed. So rare in fact that some presume it's nothing more than an urban legend."

"I need to find out as much about that film as possible. Who do I talk to?"

"Go to the Columbia Theater on Broadway."

"The Columbia Theater? That old eyesore? I thought that place was abandoned."

"Looks can be deceiving. Every night they screen rare films to an exclusive audience. Knock on the front door. When they ask you for the password say, McGuffin. Once inside, ask to see the projectionist."

The Columbia Theater looked worse than I remembered. At one time it must have been a magnificent sight with its towering sign and elaborate marquee, but nowadays it was raggedy, rundown and on the verge of collapse. I was half surprised when someone actually answered the door when I knocked.

"What's the password?"

"McGuffin."

With that the door opened, I stepped into the theater and my jaw dropped. The interior of the theater was the exact opposite of the exterior. It was immaculate. Bright red, crushed velvet carpet draped every conceivable walkway. The walls were covered in vintage movie posters. The domed ceilings allowed plenty of space for the massive glass chandeliers. I could hear the rat-a-tat of popcorn coming to life followed by the buttery aroma.

"The theater is this way sir."

The usher was dressed in a fancy red jacket and bowtie. He was walking me toward the main theater doors, but I stopped him.

"I just need to see the projectionist."

The usher pointed me to a winding staircase just off of the lobby. I followed the stairs up to a metal swinging door and entered the projectionist's booth. The clicking chatter of the film running and the loud hum of the projector made my ears buzz. The room reeked of stale smoke.

"Who the hell are you?"

The whiney voice belonged to a spindly man in his late 30's. His greasy hair was parted down the middle. He wore thick, black eye glasses that were held together by tape at the center. He was sweating profusely as he puffed enthusiastically on a cigarette.

"I want to know everything there is to know about The Creature from the Black Forest."

The projectionist eyed me suspiciously for a moment before speaking.

"What's in it for me?"

"What if I told you, I know who has it?"

I saw the projectionist's eyes light up with fervor for a brief moment. He tried not to be too obvious about his interest in the supposed cursed film, but he was failing.

"Pull up a chair."

I did so and the projectionist gave me the lowdown.

"I eat, sleep and breathe movies. Movies are my life. They are what I live for. I've seen every movie ever made no matter how rare…except for The Creature from the Black Forest."

"Do you know what it's about?"

"It's a cheesy 1970's horror flick. Nobody would have taken any interest in it if it weren't for what happened."

"And what was it that happened?"

"The movie only played in two movie theaters. It opened to a handful of people in Waukegan, Illinois. When the usher entered the theater after the movie ended, the theater was empty. The screen was white and the audience had vanished. The projectionist was missing too. No signs of any funny business, but none of those people were ever seen again."

The skinny projectionist moved in closer to me as he continued.

"Two days later the movie was shown at a little theater in downtown Greenville, Kentucky. And the same thing happened. The movie ended and the audience was gone. They too were never seen or heard from again. Nobody knows what happened to them. But there was a survivor."

"A survivor?"

"A man named Dalton bought a ticket to the movie. He said there were about a dozen people in the theater. He took a seat in the back row and the movie started. He said it was strange. All he saw was a close shot of a dark forest. There were no pre-movie credits. There was no title. Just a slightly jittery, grainy colored shot of that creepy, dark forest. It was stuck on that one shot for so long, he assumed the film had malfunctioned, so he thought that would be a good time to visit the rest room. As he was reentering the theater, he heard a loud scream. Assuming something interesting was happening on the screen, he hurried inside."

The projectionist took a long pause which I assumed was just for dramatic effect.

"Nobody was in there. The audience was gone. But the movie was still playing. It was that same shot of the forest. He claims he heard someone scream and that it sounded as if it was coming from within the movie screen! And then he saw something inside the theater. Something big. Hulking. It was coming for him, so he ran out of the theater."

The projectionist took a few more substantial puffs from his cigarette.

"Dalton died shortly after in his sleep. Legend has it he died from the constant nightmares he had from that day in the theater."

"That's quite the story."

"That's it. Now you know as much about the elusive film as I do. The one and only print of the movie has been floating around out there, changing hands from rare dealer to rare dealer. I have no clue where the film is now, but apparently you do. So please, enlighten me."

I grinned.

"I have it. Would you like to watch it?"

I took the only existing print of the film to the Columbia Theater on Broadway and the projectionist loaded it up in the projector. One press of a button and the movie would begin.

The dangers of watching the cursed movie were not lost on the projectionist, but he insisted he was willing to risk his life to see it.

Our plan was simple. As the projectionist watched the movie in the theater he would relay everything he was experiencing through a walkie-talkie. I'd be standing just outside the theater doors ready to rush in at a moment's notice at any sign of duress.

As I stood outside the theater door my heart began to accelerate when I heard the clicking of the film beginning and could see light from the theater screen flickering under the door. The projectionist's tinny voice rang through over the walkie.

"The movie has started. It's just as Dalton described. No opening credits. No title card. Just a gloomy shot of a dark forest…wait a minute…holy shit!"

I burst through the theater door with my .38 revolver in hand just after hearing the projectionist let out a cry of despair. The flickering of the lights from the screen had me disoriented and it took a few seconds for my eyes to adjust. When they finally did, I saw it. It was a mammoth, shadowy beast holding the projectionist under its arm like a ragdoll. I aimed my gun at the creature and was about to pull the trigger when it jumped into the movie screen and disappeared.

What the hell?

I dashed down the theater aisle and rushed to the screen. As I got closer, I realized that the screen was no longer solid. It was shimmering like ripples on a lake.

I reached out and touched the screen and my hunch was confirmed. It was liquid. I slowly sank my hand into the liquid mass and watched it disappear. I pushed farther until my entire arm was submerged into the screen. I was rather surprised that my arm didn't feel wet as if dunking it into a pool of water. It was dry and I could feel a gentle breeze blowing against it.

The movie created some kind of portal into its world!

"Help me!"

The anguished, distant cry of the projectionist expedited my actions and I jumped into the screen. And there I was, standing in front of the black forest.

I turned around and eyed the movie screen that was out of place in the middle of the forest. I noticed with each passing second, the shimmering screen seemed to be slightly dissolving inward. That's when it dawned on me. The screen was the door back into my world, but it would only remain there during the duration of the film, which I knew was 83 minutes.

"Help!"

The projectionist's voice was getting farther away, so I high tailed it through the endless black forest until I reached the mouth of a mammoth cave. The cave smelled like death. At the foot of the entrance was a pile of human bones. These had to be the bodies of the movie goers the creature abducted from the two theaters all those years ago.

With my .38 in hand, I began venturing deep within the dark cave using my trusty zippo lighter to light the way. I occasionally checked my wrist watch to gauge the time. My 83 minute window was closing fast. I was about to call out for the projectionist when I saw something strange.

Something large and white was propped up against the cave wall. It was approximately six feet tall. It was fluffy, like white cotton candy. I was a few feet away from it when I realized what it was.

A cocoon.

As I looked at the curious sight, I noticed that the cocoon seemed to be breathing. I could see the rhythmic swelling of the chest area and could actually hear the shallow breath. That's when I realized, it wasn't the cocoon that was breathing. It was what was inside the cocoon!

I quickly ripped the fluffy, sticky web-like substance away and found myself staring into a human face. A face I recognized from a photo Miss Kerber had given me. It was Rhett Dashwood and he was alive!

As I pulled the cocoon away from his body, Mr. Dashwood began to cough and slowly opened his eyes. His voice was hoarse when he attempted to speak.

"Who…who are you?"

I didn't have a chance to answer him due to the clomping of footsteps rushing our way from deep within the bowels of the cave. I carefully aimed my revolver and was about to squeeze the trigger when the projectionist came bolting into view.

"We have to get out of here! It's coming!"

My eyes widened with fear as the creature from the Black Forest emerged from the shadows. The beast was gigantic. At least 8 feet tall. It looked like a cross between a gorilla and a spider. Its legs were stout and brawny. Its torso was muscular. It had six long, slender, hairy arms. The creature's face was round, bushy and housed two beady red eyes. The beast had massive jaws that snapped open and closed from the sides.

"Go! Save yourselves. I'll delay it!"

I was shocked by the projectionist's suggestion.

"We're in this together buddy! I'm not leaving you behind."

"We won't make it! It will chase us down and kill all of us. But if I can fight it off for a few minutes, you two might be able to survive! Movies are my life. And now I'm going to die inside of one. There's something poetic about that."

He didn't give me a chance to argue. He gave me a shove, picked up a large club-like stick and began attacking the gigantic creature with it.

I grabbed Rhett Dashwood, wrapped his arm around my shoulders to steady him and we rushed through the terrifying Black Forest. It was a few minutes later when I heard the projectionist let forth with a death cry. That was followed by the heavy footsteps of the creature giving chase and it was closing in rapidly. The creature had gained so much ground on us that I could actually hear it's ghastly, wheezing breath and smell its foul musky odor.

I was expecting the beast to reach out at any second and grab us when I saw the screen! At that point it was the size of a modest television screen and it was shrinking quickly. I could see reversed credits rolling on the screen. The movie was over. In just a few seconds the screen was going to evaporate and we'd be stuck in the Black Forest for the creature to devour at its leisure.

"Jump!"

I shouted out the instructions to Mr. Dashwood. Whether he tagged along or not was up to him but I was taking my shot. I hurled myself through the tiny opening that the screen had reduced to and found myself on the floor of the Columbia Theater. A second later, Rhett Dashwood came barreling through the screen.

All at once the clicking of the film stopped and the theater went dark. The movie was over. We had managed to slink our way through the screen just as it was evaporating. We had successfully escaped the Black Forest and were safe and sound back in our own world.

Simone Kerber was ecstatic to see her fiancé alive and well. The couple paid me my full fee, plus a hefty bonus for a job well done.

I tossed the only print of *The Creature from the Black Forest* onto a blazing fire and took pleasure in watching it disintegrate. I slept well that night.

Just another day on the job.

THE CHEATER
The Boyfriend

My name is Terry. I'm a senior in high school and I have the best girlfriend in the world. Her name is Tina. She's all any guy could ever ask for.

First of all, she's a real looker. She possesses stunning natural beauty. She could be a model if she wanted to. But her dream is to own her own clothing store. She loves to sew and makes most of her own garments.

I'm big into sports. This is a turn off for some of the girls at our school, but not Tina. She's a sports fan as much as I am and we both root for the same teams. I can have sports related conversations with her for hours. It's so great!

Whenever I'm in a bad mood, Tina is always there to cheer me up. She takes genuine interest in what is ailing me and does whatever she can to remedy the situation. But the fact is, just having her in my arms is enough to cure any of my woes.

Tina is perfect! She's so fun to be with. When we're apart I count the seconds until we're together again and each time I see her she takes my breath away just as though I'm seeing her for the first time all over again.

My best friend is named Chuck. He's the captain of the football team and is the big man on campus. Even though he's dating the head cheerleader, he's constantly telling me how lucky I am to have a girl like Tina. He's always complaining about his girlfriends and their list of incompatibilities with him. I remember him once saying that he wished he had a girlfriend like Tina.

It was a Friday afternoon. I was looking forward to seeing Tina. We had a date the previous night that she had to cancel because she said she didn't feel well. I was anxious to see her and to find out if she was feeling better.

As I was about to round the corner of the hallway, I heard Tina's cheerful voice cry out.

"Hi Chuck!"

I stopped and slowly peeked around the corner. Tina and Chuck were standing by her locker. They were both all smiles. My heart sank when I heard Tina's words.

"I'm so glad you could come over last night. Can you come over again tonight?"

Chuck was over at Tina's house last night? She told me she was sick! As their conversation continued everything became quite clear.

"Don't you think Terry might get suspicious?"

"No. I told him I wasn't feeling well last night. I'll use that excuse again."

Tina was cheating on me with my best friend. I couldn't believe it.

I left school early that day and spent the evening sulking in my room. It didn't seem real. I couldn't believe the two people who I trusted more than anyone would do something like that to me.

When Tina called me to tell me she had to break our date because she still wasn't feeling well, it was confirmed. And my heart didn't just sink. It disappeared. I became enraged and insanity began flowing through my veins.

I didn't want to live if I couldn't have Tina. And if I couldn't have her, nobody could, especially my former best friend!

I grabbed my father's shotgun from the wall and marched down the street to Tina's house. I stood on the front porch and peered in through the window.

There they were. Chuck's back was to me. He was holding his arms out to the side as he prepared to embrace my girlfriend. Tina was giddy and was running her hands over Chuck's chest.

I erupted.

I walked to the front door of Tina's house and kicked the door open. Tina and Chuck spun around with shocked expressions. I shot Tina first, but wasted no time in shooting Chuck as well.

I stared down at their dead bodies for a few seconds and cried before I dropped to my knees, put the barrel of the shotgun in my mouth and pulled the trigger.

THE CHEATER
The Girlfriend

My name is Tina and I love my boyfriend Terry more than anything. I just know we'll spend the rest of our lives together and live happily ever after.

I hated deceiving Terry. I truly did, but it was necessary. I was sure he would understand.

I was sewing a sweater for Terry with his favorite football team's emblem on it. I knew he would love it, but I needed someone to use as a model to make sure I got the measurements correct. Chuck and Terry are roughly the same size and Chuck was nice enough to help me out.

I thought I would just need Chuck to come over one night, but to be on the safe side I had him come out on Friday night as well. He was such a good sport, holding his arms out to the side while I held Terry's soon to be completed sweater against his chest and took measurements.

I was looking forward to not only seeing Terry's face when he saw the sweater I made for him, but also in letting him know why I misled him.

In the end, I was certain that it would all work out fine.

THE OUIJA BOARD

When my girlfriend Samantha passed away unexpectedly, I was devastated. Nobody saw it coming. She was only 27 years old, was athletically fit, yet died suddenly from heart failure. I remembered asking the doctor how something like this could happen and his response was "One can never predict cardiac arrest."

Samantha's sister Nicole took it hard too. It would be an understatement to say the two sisters didn't get along. They couldn't be in the same room for more than an hour without getting into an argument. But in the end, they were still sisters.

Nicole and I spent a lot of time together after Samantha's passing. We grieved together and grew quite close. She was a horticulturist and the array of flowers she kept in her house emitted a soothing explosion of colors which always made me feel comforted. For a long while, I used those flowers as an excuse to visit Nicole. Eventually I could no longer deny the fact that it was my newfound feelings for her that had me returning again and again.

I have to admit that I felt guilty when we started seeing each other. At first I thought it was because Nicole reminded me of Samantha. They shared the same ice blue eyes and curly blonde hair. They both displayed dimples when they smiled and their laugh was nearly identical.

Eventually I realized that my feelings for Nicole went far deeper than that. I truly loved her for who she was, not for who she reminded me of. But still, the demise of Samantha being the sole reason that I found happiness with her sister wasn't easy for me to live with.

Nicole was sweet and understanding. I could tell her anything and if I was troubled she was great at cheering me up. She suggested that I try to keep my mind focused on things I enjoy while I allowed time to pass and heal my wounds.

One of my favorite things to do was to visit an antique store down the road from my house every Friday just after they set out their latest items. I liked old, unusual things. My apartment was decorated with an assortment of vintage pieces and I was always looking for more to add to my collection.

I hadn't visited the store since Samantha died, so the majority of their items would be new to my eye. I'd likely spend the entire day there, but that was exactly what I needed.

I picked up a few rare glass figurines that were made in Japan, a drive-in movie speaker and some rusty Coca-Cola advertising. As I was checking out, an old, wooden Ouija board hanging on the wall behind the store owner caught my eye.

It was quite unusual. Like the mass produced Ouija boards that most people are familiar with, this had the words "yes" and "no" at the top. The center of the board was dominated by every letter in the alphabet and numerical numbers were positioned under them. At the bottom of the board was the word, "goodbye." But that was where the similarity to the mass produced boards ended.

This wooden Ouija board was quite thick and cherry stained. The letters and numbers were elegantly carved into the wood. A matching wooden heart shaped planchette dangled by a chain from the board. Even though the Ouija board was in fantastic condition, it was obvious that this hadn't been made recently.

"What can you tell me about that Ouija board?"

The old store owner put his spectacles on as he turned around and eyed the impressive block of wood.

"That's the real deal there. That's not the kind of Ouija board you pick up at the five-and-dime. That's authentic. Late 1800's."

When he rattled off the cost to purchase the board I didn't hesitate with my response.

"Sold!"

After taking my money and handing me the Ouija board, the store owner leaned in and spoke seriously.

"Be careful with this, son. This isn't a toy to be played with. It's a true portal that can bring forth things into this world that shouldn't be here."

I heeded his warning. I had no intention of being mischievous with the board. I simply wanted to display its beauty, thus I hung it up in a prominent location in my apartment.

Nicole didn't see the attractiveness in it that I did. She couldn't understand what I saw in it and was surprised not only that I had purchased it, but that I hung it up as a display piece.

We settled in on the couch and began watching a romantic comedy. We weren't halfway into the movie when we began kissing and things were getting rather passionate, but Nicole kept pausing to look back at the Ouija board. Eventually she shook her head and stood up.

"I can't do this tonight."

"What's wrong?"

Nicole pointed at the Ouija board.

"I don't like that thing. It gives off a bad vibe. I feel like we're being watched!"

She suggested we continue things at her house the following night and left abruptly. I sat there staring at the Ouija board. I didn't feel any negative energy and certainly didn't feel like I was being watched. However, when I went to bed that night, I was surprised to find a t-shirt belonging to Samantha splayed out on my bed.

Samantha had several clothing items at my apartment and after she died I couldn't bring myself to part with them, so they were still hanging in the corner of my closet.

But why was this one on my bed?

The shirt in question was a teal t-shirt with a dolphin on the front. Samantha bought it when we were on vacation at the beach. It was the one and only time Nicole vacationed with us. The sisters were at each other's throats the entire time. And they had argued over that shirt. They both wanted it, but it was the only one left. Eventually Nicole gave in by shouting "Fine. Take it. You always get what you want!"

I suppose it was plausible that Nicole had gone into my closet and saw the shirt. It likely brought back some bad memories. That may have been why she didn't feel like staying.

The following night I went over to Nicole's house. She made me dinner and after we ate, we sat in her heavily flowered sunroom. When I asked her if she had laid the shirt out on the bed, she was shocked.

"No of course not!"

Apparently bringing up the subject of Samantha touched a nerve.

"You still love her, don't you?"

"Samantha?"

I shrugged.

"Yes, I guess I always will."

Nicole crossed her arms and took a defensive posture as she stared silently out at the darkened sky.

"What's wrong, Nicole?"

"Last week when I spent the night at your house, I found a picture of you and Samantha in your nightstand drawer."

"Yeah, so?"

"Do you keep that picture on your nightstand and just put it in the drawer when you bring me in there to screw me? Is that how it is? Are you imagining it's her when we have sex?"

"Whoa, calm down."

"Answer me!"

"I had that picture on my nightstand the entire time Samantha and I were together. I put it in the drawer the day I started seeing you. Where is this coming from all of a sudden?"

"Something happened. I feel like she's here!"

"Who?"

"Samantha! It's like I can feel her with us right now staring at me disapprovingly."

"Nicole, that's crazy…"

"Just go. Go home. Leave me alone!"

Nicole got up, stormed to her bedroom and slammed the door shut. This was all very strange, but rather than make things worse by staying, I decided to go home. I was hoping the following day after she calmed down we might be able to have a civil conversation.

When I got home and began opening my apartment door, I heard a loud bang coming from my bedroom. I flicked on the lights, rushed to my bedroom and froze when I saw it.

My nightstand drawer was open. The picture of me and Samantha was shattered on the floor. That's when I heard a loud crash from the living room. When I hurried in there to see what happened, I found the Ouija board lying on the floor. The heart shaped planchette was sitting on the center of the board and suddenly began moving around all by itself.

I stood in total shock as I watched the planchette move sharply from letter to letter.

S-I-S-T-E-R

"Sister? Samantha, is that you?"

The planchette quickly scooted to the word, YES and then slid back to the alphabet and rapidly spelled out another word.

O-L-E-A-N-D-E-R

"Oleander?"

Suddenly the planchette flew from the board and rocketed toward me. I shielded my face with my hands as it slammed against me and then dropped to the floor.

I was scared, I was freaking out and I felt like I was losing my mind. I ran out of the apartment, jumped in my car and floored it back to Nicole's house. I had to tell her what happened. Maybe together we could communicate with Samantha and figure this out.

I hurried to Nicole's front door and knocked. She answered and looked happy to see me. A smile came across her face and I got the impression that she was going to apologize for her behavior earlier that night, but I jumped in and spoke first.

"Do you know what oleander means?"

Upon hearing the word, Nicole's smile vanished and the blood drained from her face. She was silent for a long moment.

"How did you find out?"

I didn't know what she was talking about. I was about to ask her what she meant when she continued.

"Oleander is the toxic plant I used to poison Samantha with. It was the only way I could have you.

I've been in love with you ever since we all took that trip to the beach together."

It took a minute for the meaning of her words to make sense to me. Then I fell to my knees and broke down.

Nicole confessed everything to the police.

When I finally got back to my apartment that night I found the planchette sitting in the middle of the Ouija board. I watched on with sadness as it slowly moved down to the word "goodbye."

SOMETHING WICKED THIS WAY COMES

In 1974, Possum Trot, Kentucky was an old-fashioned, peaceful little town. It was the kind of town that you could leave your doors unlocked and windows open without giving it a second thought.

Everyone did their shopping downtown. At the General Store, Mrs. Fletcher would greet customers with a smile and was always quick to help anyone find what they needed. Mr. Otis ran the Corner Candy Store and gave me a handful of tootsie rolls for free when I bought something. My favorite store downtown was Walker's Pet Store. They always had puppies, kittens and rabbits. Sweet Miss Walker would let me play with them for hours on end. She even let me name my favorite animals. My favorite rabbits were Bonnie and Clyde, my favorite kittens were Chip and Dale and my two favorite dogs were Zig and Zag.

Every Sunday the townsfolk would gather at the church and enjoy the service given by Reverend Tucker. Afterward everyone would meet in the parking lot for the weekly town barbeque. Everybody knew each other and cared for one another. It was like the town was one big family. Living there was pleasant to say the least.

I was ten years old when Doc Weaver retired. That's when things in the town started to change…and not for the better. The change I speak of coincided with the arrival of the new town doctor. His name was Dr. Wolfe.

Dr. Wolfe was tall and slender. He wore a black top hat and dark gray cloak over his black suit. He was a man in his early 60's with sharp features and a contoured black beard. He carried himself with quiet confidence and the townsfolk were instantly enamored of him.

When I first met him at the weekly town barbeque he seemed friendly enough. He said that I looked like a fine chap and patted my head. My initial opinion of him began to change when he smiled. His teeth were stained yellow likely from years of tobacco use and his eye teeth were pointed, animal-like and intimidating.

It was when I looked into his eyes that I began to fear Dr. Wolfe. The colors of his eyes were so cold and gloomy. I could see my own reflection within them as if I was staring into a black pond. There was something sinister behind those wicked eyes that he couldn't hide regardless of the friendly façade he presented.

Later that week my parents went shopping downtown. They spent most of their time at the General Store and allowed me to venture off on my own. My first stop was the Corner Candy Store. I wanted to get a brick of fudge. Peanut butter was my favorite and was always what I intended to buy, but Mr. Otis had such a variety of flavors, I often changed my mind.

When I entered the Corner Candy Store, I saw Dr. Wolfe at the counter speaking to Mr. Otis. The fudge display was across the store, so I was too far away to hear what Dr. Wolfe was saying clearly, but I could hear his mumbles. They were constant. He was speaking a lot and Mr. Otis was listening intently.

Eventually Dr. Wolfe stopped talking. When he turned and began walking toward the exit door, I could see that he had purchased a bag of black licorice. He was chewing on a piece when he noticed me. He didn't slow down upon seeing me. He simply winked at me as he strolled out of the store.

When I stepped to the counter to inform Mr. Otis of my fudge selection, I noticed he wasn't paying attention to me at all. He was staring at the door Dr. Wolfe had just exited through. He seemed as though he were in some kind of a daze.

"Mr. Otis?"

Upon hearing my voice, Mr. Otis shook his head slightly and took my order, but his head still seemed to be in the clouds. He wasn't smiling or being the friendly person he normally was. He seemed preoccupied. And that was the first day Mr. Otis didn't give me a handful of free tootsie rolls.

My next stop was Walker's Pet Store. When I entered the store, I was surprised to see Dr. Wolfe again. He was standing at the register holding my two favorite rabbits, Bonnie and Clyde, by the nape of their necks in a not so delicate manner. When he spotted me staring at the rabbits, he addressed me.

"Don't worry boy. I'll take good care of them."

His voice was deep and callous. I did not feel reassured as he exited the store with the bunnies.

As I approached Miss Walker, she was acting in a similar fashion as Mr. Otis was. She was staring at the door. Her eyes were glazed over. Her mind was elsewhere.

"Miss Walker?"

She blinked her eyes a few times and then looked down at me. She did not speak in a friendly tone.

"What do you want?"

"Can I play with Zig and Zag?

Miss Walker shook her head.

"Not today. Go on, go find your parents. I'm closing the store early. Scoot!"

Miss Walker quickly ushered me out of the store, shut the door behind me and flipped her store sign to "closed."

Over the next few weeks, I saw Dr. Wolfe walking through town often. The townsfolk would stop and gawk at him as if in awe as he passed by and tipped his hat at them. It was like he was some kind of rock star in their eyes. I didn't get it.

Over the next few months, the attendance at Sunday church service gradually decreased. Normally it was standing room only, but with each passing week, less people showed. One week the church was three quarters full. The next week only half full. A few weeks later it was down to one quarter full. Then one Sunday afternoon when we stepped through the church doors, there were only three other people there.

The weekly town barbeques had become a thing of the past as well. And I noticed that the townsfolk weren't as happy and kind as they once were. They were all becoming emotionless and deadpanned. Mr. Otis still operated the Corner Candy Store, but he wasn't friendly anymore. He just took my money and handed me my candy.

The worst day for me was when I walked into Walker's Pet Store and Zig & Zag were gone. Then I noticed Chip and Dale were gone. As a matter of fact, the entire store was void of pets. I asked Miss Walker where the animals were and she said she sold them all. I asked who bought them and she told me it was none of my business and kicked me out.

When I exited the pet store, I saw Dr. Wolfe driving away from the store in a black van. I could hear distressed barking coming from within.

While the weekly town barbeques stopped happening, the townsfolk still got together every week. At Dr. Wolfe's house. He lived in the largest house in the area. It was located on top of a hill and overlooked the entire town. On Sunday nights people gathered at his house for some kind of town meeting. And one of the kids at school told me that his parents started going to some sort of church service that Dr. Wolfe held at his home.

One night after dinner, as my parents were doing the dishes, I heard them talking about Dr. Wolfe. They were chatting about going to one of Dr. Wolfe's sermons. They were both reluctant but apparently the rest of the townsfolk were pressuring them to attend.

I asked them if I could go with them, but they said no. They explained that Dr. Wolfe's church service was held at midnight and that children weren't allowed.

Midnight? Why would anyone hold a service so late? Why didn't they want kids to attend? These were major red flags for me, why weren't they for everyone else?

That night, I pretended like I was asleep and then followed my parents to Dr. Wolfe's large home. The whole town was there. I watched from afar and waited until they all entered his house before I snuck up closer.

I peeked in through the kitchen window, but didn't spot anyone. I moved around the front of the house and peered in through the living room window, but couldn't see a soul.

Where were they?

That's when I noticed the exterior cellar doors near the side of the house. I could see the flickering of light emitting through the cracks. As I approached them I could hear unison group chanting coming from inside.

I slowly, carefully opened one of the cellar doors just enough for me to slide my body through. I found myself at the top of a flight of crude concrete stairs. I stealthily stepped down the stairs, making sure I kept myself hidden in the shadows.

The basement was enormous and primitive. The floor was dirt. There were wooden shelves lining the walls. Many of the shelves housed clear jars that held some type of red liquid. Oh how I hoped it was jam.

I snuck up closer to the congregation of people and hid behind a large whiskey barrel.

All of the townsfolk were wearing black robes with the hoods up, shielding their faces. They were standing in rows facing Dr. Wolfe who was in front of them much like Reverend Tucker would be while delivering church service.

Dr. Wolfe was dressed in an identical cloak as the congregation, with the exception of his being dark red in color. He was standing in the center of a large five pointed star that was painted on the cellar floor and encircled with large, blistering candles.

Behind Dr. Wolfe were cages upon cages of the animals from the pet store. I could see the puppies, Zig and Zag, near the front. They were shivering with fear. The kittens, Chip and Dale were hissing at Dr.

Wolfe as he spoke and the bunnies, Bonnie and Clyde were hopping around nervously in their cage.

The congregation chanted for several minutes until Dr. Wolfe held up his hands at which time they immediately fell silent. He spoke several words in a language I was not familiar with before he began giving a sermon.

What he was saying didn't make any sense to me. He spoke of darkness consuming all, giving oneself to temptation, the spilling of innocent blood and live sacrifices.

Dr. Wolfe then stepped to the bunny cage and removed Bonnie. He held her by the nape of her neck, raised her high into the air and then unsheathed a gigantic knife from under his cloak and held it against Bonnie's throat.

"Nooo!"

I rocketed through the center of the congregation, rushed up to Dr. Wolfe and slammed into him with all of my might. He fell to the ground and dropped Bonnie in the process. As she hopped away to safety, I quickly opened all of the cage doors and set the animals free.

Dr. Wolfe was frothing at the mouth as he pointed at me.

"Catch that little son of a bitch! Kill him!"

The townsfolk started looking around at each other and I could hear a slight murmur as they began speaking, questioning Dr. Wolfe's order. They weren't fully under his spell. Not yet. But I wasn't going to wait around for them to change their minds. I ran to the cellar doors, flung them open and ran with the animals to safety.

When I got home my parents were in the kitchen. My mother was on the phone in tears as my father listened on closely. They were worried and searching for me, no doubt. But I wasn't going to let them know of my whereabouts. Not yet. I had something to take care of first.

I quietly crept into my parents' bedroom and removed my father's double barrel shotgun from above the door. I then made my way back to Dr. Wolfe's house.

I waited outside his house for over an hour until all of the townsfolk's vehicles were gone and then I snuck back into the basement through the cellar doors.

Dr. Wolfe was alone. He was no longer wearing his red robe. He was donning his normal black suit and was sitting in a chair at the center of the five pointed star. His eyes were closed and he was whispering something to himself.

I was silent as I cautiously moved within ten feet of the sinister man. His eyes shot open when he heard me cock the gun.

"Leave my town now or I'll pull this trigger and blow your head off."

Dr. Wolfe showed no fear whatsoever as he stared down the barrel of the gun.

"I see you hold a darkness within, much as I do."

I spoke sharply so that there was no misunderstanding.

"I'm nothing like you. I'm simply defending my peaceful town against a wicked, evil thing."

He stared coldly at me for a long moment contemplating his options. Finally he let out a defeated breath and spoke.

"Fine you brave boy. I'll leave your town. But you can't stop me. Over the next fifty years you'll witness the steady decline of civilization the world over as I sink my hooks in deeper and deeper."

"That's the world's problem. I just want to save my little town."

Dr. Wolfe smirked before he placed his top hat on his head, fastened his cloak over his black suit and left town.

It took several months, but gradually the town woke from its stupor and eventually everything went back to normal. The townsfolk were happy, cheerful and friendly. Mr. Otis started giving me free tootsie rolls with every order again. Miss Walker let me play with all of the animals at the pet store. The church was standing room only and the town barbeque was bigger and better than ever.

I couldn't save the world, but I did manage to save my little town.

IS CHIVALRY DEAD?

It wasn't the best place in the world for the average person to be broken down. It was a desolate location with spotty cell service at best. The freshly laid black asphalt certainly didn't mean the road got much in the way of traffic. From my estimation a car passed by once every hour.

Definitely not the best spot to be broken down. Especially for a woman.

I'm tall and thin with bushy blonde hair. Most consider me to be an attractive lady. Normally I don't have trouble getting people to stop for me if I look like I need assistance, but today was different. Here I sat in the driver's seat of my car with the door open and the hood up, and three cars had zoomed past me without even slowing down to see if I needed some help. Two of the three people were men.

Maybe chivalry *was* dead.

That was the very thought coursing through my brain when another vehicle rounded the bend, but unlike the others, this one slowed as it passed by.

It was a rusty, old pickup truck. I could see that there was only one person in the vehicle. It was a man. He had a scruffy appearance. He slowed enough to gawk at me with a stern expression.

He continued past me, like the others. I was surprised when suddenly his brake lights lit up like a beacon and he screeched to a halt. He just sat there for a moment before his white reverse lights illuminated the road and he slowly backed up to my car. His door let forth with a rusty creak as he slowly pushed it open and stepped out.

The man was husky and was wearing a thick, dirty jacket and an oil stained ball cap. His long unkempt beard was peppered with small splotches of gray patches. His eyes were dark and highlighted by deep creases. I noticed a large, ugly scar over his left eye and he held his mouth in a snarl. As he stepped toward me, I thought I noticed him looking me up and down, but that could have been my imagination. He spoke with a gruff voice.

"Car trouble?"

I glanced at the open hood and back at him.

"How'd you guess?"

The man took a few more steps and stopped when he was just a few feet from me. I was mistaken about his eyes. From a distance they appeared dark and cold, but up close they were ocean-blue and friendly. I was surprised when a beaming smile broke over his roughened face. It was so bright and welcoming. It instantly put me at ease. His voice softened with the smile.

"I have to be honest. I don't know much about cars. But I'd be happy to call someone for you or give you a lift somewhere."

I smiled back at him.

"It's okay. My car isn't really broken down."

He crinkled his brow in confusion and never even noticed as I reached around my back and removed my handy hatchet from its holster. He didn't suspect a thing as I whacked him in the face with it.

The blade didn't drive too deep into his face, but the blow knocked him silly and he staggered for a few seconds before falling to the ground. I instantly jumped on top of him and brought the hatchet down.

"It used to be so easy to get men to stop to help me."

I chopped into his face again.

"Nowadays, you'd be surprised how many just drive right by without any consideration to stop and help a lady in distress."

I continued hacking away.

"Maybe some of them thought this was some kind of a scam for me to get them to stop so I could rob them…or kill them. And they'd be correct."

I stopped my assault once his face was unrecognizable and I could see chunks of his skull protruding through the mangled flesh.

"Maybe chivalry isn't dead after all."

TAKEN

I was four days away from being 16 years old. I couldn't wait. The first thing I was going to do was get my driver's license. My parents had already bought me a car. I just needed my license and I'd be all set. And I wasn't the only one looking forward to me getting my license. My parents were too.

I was a hard working girl. I was able to get a job as a cashier at a movie theater when I turned 15. But the theater was a thirty minute drive from my house, thus my parents had to drive me to and from. They'd be thrilled once they didn't have to chauffeur me around anymore.

The other primary beneficiary would be my best friend, Holly. Holly had another six months to go before she turned 16 and got her own license. But in the meantime I'd be happy to let her tag along with me to school and back. Our dreary bus riding days were almost over!

Holly lived just down the block from me. The bus always dropped us off at the entrance of a long, gloomy alleyway. Our parents had warned us not to use the alley as a short cut, but it cut our walking time down by half, so of course we were going to use that alley to save that precious time!

It was a Monday afternoon. The bus had dropped us off and we were using the alley shortcut when Holly pointed out a suspicious white van parked against the back of a store. She called it a "rapist" van and said the only thing missing were the words "free candy" written on the side. I laughed at her joke and paranoia. I didn't think the van was suspicious. My dad was a locksmith and drove a similar van, except his was blue and had his company name plastered all over it. This one was very plain and had no windows in the back.

Holly insisted we give it a wide berth as we walked past it. That seemed reasonable and we did just that. The van was there again on Tuesday. We kept our distance from it then too. By the time Wednesday rolled around and the van was once again in the same vicinity, we assumed it to be owned by an employee of one of the businesses it was parked behind. By Thursday, it was just a natural part of the scenery and we didn't bat an eye when we walked by it.

On Friday, Holly called me before I left for the bus stop to inform me that she was ill and would not be going to school that day. She asked if I'd pick up any homework she needed and I did so.

When I got off the bus that afternoon, I contemplated taking the longer, safer route home since I was all alone, but it was my 16th birthday and my mom was waiting at home to take me to get my driver's license so I wasn't going to waste a second!

The only thing on my mind as I meandered down the alley that day was my driver's test. I was ultra-confident that I would ace it. It was the final hurdle to getting my driver's license. I was more anxious than I was nervous.

I didn't even realize that I was walking by the white, windowless van, so I startled when I heard the side door slide open with vigor. Just as the door opened, I felt two sets of hands grab me and pull me inside. I started screaming as I heard the door to the van close behind me. Within a second, the engine roared to life and I could hear the tires screeching as it tore out of the alley.

My assailants immediately put a burlap sack over my head while simultaneously jabbing a syringe into my arm. Within seconds, I blacked out.

I don't know how much time had gone by when I groggily opened my eyes. My vision was blurred, but I could see daylight breaking through some of the tiny gaps in the rustic, burlap material. I was extremely weak. I could barely move a muscle, but I could hear two men talking to each other.

"How old do you think she is?"

"15 or 16."

"You know we'll get a lot more for her if her hymen is still intact."

"I know. They'll check her out before they bring her up."

The conversation I was hearing was terrifying. I tried to scream, but in my weakened state, I only let out a frail mumble.

"She's waking up. Give her another injection."

Upon feeling a sting in my arm, I blacked out again.

When I woke up, I could tell that the burlap sack had been removed from my head, but I now had a thick blindfold over my eyes. I could feel strong hands under my arms holding me up into a standing position. I had minimal strength in my legs. Whenever I tried to stand on my own, my legs felt like wet spaghetti.

I could feel the strong man holding me and parading me around. He was walking back and forth and would occasionally spin me. I could detect an audience of some kind in front of me. The air was filled with the constant buzz of voices. I heard a microphone pop on and an amplified voice begin speaking to the room of spectators.

"Here we have a female in the 14 to 16 age range. She's 5' 3" and approximately 115 pounds. As you can see she has blonde hair and our medical team can confirm that she is virgin pure. Who'll start the bidding at thirty thousand dollars?"

I couldn't believe what I was hearing! I was being auctioned off at some kind of perverted sale. I tried to scream out, but was only able to produce incoherent grumbling which certainly couldn't be heard over the bidding war that was taking place.

"Fifty thousand!"

"Sixty thousand!"

"Eighty thousand!"

There were a variety of voices shouting out bids. Mostly men, but I distinctly heard at least two different women as well. Within a matter of minutes, the auction had concluded.

"Sold to the distinguished gentleman for one hundred and twenty thousand dollars!"

Again, I felt a sharp stab in my arm and I passed out.

I woke up to the feeling of swaying back and forth. I could hear water splashing up against the side of whatever I was in. I slowly opened my eyes and for the first time since being taken, I could see. I had no sack over my head. I had no blindfold on. And the sight before my eyes was horrifying.

I was lying down in a small cage that was barely big enough to house me. After a few blinks the blurriness of my vision cleared up and I felt strength in my body. I stood up, but had to hunch slightly to keep my head from hitting the top of the cage.

I was in a large, dim metal room. And I wasn't alone. There were at least a dozen more cages within the room. Each cage contained a young girl my age or younger. They were lying unconscious in their cages, but I could see them breathing. I must have been the first one to wake up.

I wasn't sure exactly where I was, but I knew I had to get out of there fast!

I tried to push the cage door open, but not surprisingly it was locked. I reached my hand through the cage and felt for the locking mechanism on the door. I was relieved to find that it was a very basic lock. I ran my fingers through my hair and prayed that I could find a bobby pin. My prayers were answered when I found one tucked deep into the back of my frazzled hair.

At a very young age, I took interest in my father's profession and my proud dad taught me a thing or two about the locksmith business. I could pick most basic locks with my eyes closed. The cage I found myself enclosed in was no exception. Within a matter of minutes, I had the cage door opened and I stepped into the middle of the cold, dingy room.

As I gazed about, I spotted the door. It was a large cargo type door. There was light emanating from under the crack at the bottom and I could see movement outside. I hurried to the door and pressed my ear to it hoping to hear something that may give me a clue as to where I was. I could distinctly overhear two men having a conversation.

"Fantasy Island here we come."

"The big wigs are going to have themselves a time at the gala tonight."

"You got that right. They're getting the cream of the crop."

"You mean they're gonna cream *on* that crop!"

As the men chuckled, I heard the door to the room being unlocked. I quickly pressed myself against the wall in the darkest corner of the room. I watched as the door swung open and two men stepped inside. They both wore khaki uniforms and started checking the cages.

"We just have to make sure they have enough water to last them until we reach the island."

It would only be a matter of seconds before they noticed my cage was empty and that I was gone. I had no time to waste, so I quietly crept out of the room and recognized that I was in well lit, thin corridor. There was a flight of stairs directly in front of me. I scurried up the stairs and found myself on the deck of a gigantic yacht. There were several people in khaki uniforms milling about, but none of them saw me. I was able to get on my hands and knees and hide behind a fancy, cushioned lounge chair.

The loud blare of the ship's horn startled me and I could see a khaki uniformed man begin to unfasten the thick ropes that were holding the yacht to a long pier.

I was running out of time!

I crouched down as I darted across the deck. As I passed by several windows, I could see that there was a party going on. There were a lot of men in tuxedos and women in evening gowns. They were drinking champagne and having a jolly fine time. Fortunately none of them saw me as I rushed to the edge of the yacht near where the khaki uniformed man was undoing the ropes. There was no getting off the yacht without him seeing me so I jumped right past him onto the pier and started running.

"We have a runaway! I repeat we have a runaway!"

I looked back over my shoulder and could see that the khaki dressed man was speaking into a walkie-talkie. It wasn't long before several of his cohorts had jumped from the yacht to the pier and were giving chase, but I had a healthy lead on them.

The marina I was at was huge. There were all kinds of fancy ships tied to various docks. As I reached the end of the pier I hurried to the parking lot and hid next to a parked car. Just as I ducked out of sight, two security vehicles skidded to a halt at the end of the pier. When they got out they were met by a few of the khaki uniformed men. They engaged in frantic conversation for a moment and then began searching the parking lot for me. Luckily, they started their search on the wrong side of the lot and one of the security guards made the mistake of leaving his car running and the door open.

I hurried to the car, got into the driver's seat and just barely pulled the door shut enough for the interior light to shut off. My instinct was to peel rubber out of there, but I knew such action would draw attention and I'd likely be taken all over again. I restrained that urge and slowly, quietly coasted the car out of the parking lot.

They never even noticed.

When I reached a main road, I floored it until I was miles away from the marina. I had no clue where I was, I just got on the nearest expressway and drove. I was rather shocked when I saw a sign indicating I was leaving New York State. I didn't live anywhere near New York. I guessed my home to be over 500 miles away from there!

I looked down at the gas gauge and found that I had a full tank of gas to work with. I wasn't going to stop for some time. I wanted to put distance between myself and my captors.

Once the car got down to a quarter of a tank of gas, I stopped at a police station. I told the authorities everything I knew, but it wasn't much. I didn't even know the name of the marina I was held captive at. I got the feeling that the minimal information I provided wasn't going to be enough for them to do much with.

Several hours later my parents arrived and took me home.

While I was thankful to have gotten out of that ordeal alive, I felt awful for the rest of the girls in those cages who weren't so fortunate. And there was no doubt in my mind, what I experienced was just the tip of one gigantic, deviant iceberg.

SCHOOL SHOOTER
The Teacher

I'm a history teacher at Tradewater High School located in Northern Kentucky. It was the early portion of 2nd period when the onslaught began.

At first I thought someone had set off a cluster of firecrackers as a prank, but it only took me a few seconds to recognize the sound for what it really was.

Gunfire.

The shots were being squeezed off in rapid succession and were getting closer. I rushed to the classroom door and flung it open only to see students and faculty screaming for their lives as they rushed down the hallway.

I was seconds away from ushering my students out the door when I saw the shooter. He was at the end of the hallway and heading toward us quickly. If we exited the room, we'd all be easy targets. I thought our best chance was to barricade ourselves in the room and hope the crazed shooter walked past without entering.

I didn't even have to direct my students. They all found shelter in the far corners of the room or under their desks. I stood in front of the room as a last line of defense for them.

My hopes were shattered when the door was kicked open and the shooter entered.

"Elias?"

I was shocked to see Elias Bennings standing at the entrance of the classroom. He was dressed in blue jeans, a white t-shirt and a baseball cap. He was holding a rifle in a ready position.

Elias was the last student I would expect to be shooting up the school. He was a straight A student. He had a seat on the student council and was president of the Science Fiction Club.

He was also the number one target of our worst school bully "Bad" Billy Pratt. I could only guess that Billy Pratt finally pushed Elias over the edge and he snapped.

"Move out of the way, Miss Blaire. I don't want to hurt you."

I wish I could say I stood strong as a shield for my students, but the second Elias pointed the gun at my head, I crumpled to the ground like a coward and watched on in horror as Elias began shooting kids at random.

At least I thought it was at random.

Elias didn't hesitate to fire away at the three kids closest to him, killing them instantly. But then he paused and pointed at one of the other students.

"You, get out!"

The student he singled out followed Elias's order and fled from the room free of harm. I was hoping Elias would allow the remainder of the students out, but he began firing again, taking the lives of five other students in a matter of seconds. Then, once again, Elias hesitated and began pointing at multiple students and addressing some of them by name.

"Susie, Bill, James, you all get out of here. Hurry."

When a student he didn't name tried to escape with the others, Elias singled him out.

"Not you."

He pulled the trigger and splattered the boy's head all over the room.

The pattern continued with Elias freeing some students while murdering the others until finally, he lowered his weapon, turned around and left the room.

I crawled to the door and peered out into the hallway, hopeful that Elias would exit the building, but instead he entered another room and began firing. Once again, he appeared to let several of the students leave, but killed the rest. Then he moved on to another room and another as the vicious cycle continued.

I was shocked when I saw the school's principal, Mr. Barnes rushing down the hallway towards Elias. Mr. Barnes was a robust man in his early 60's with thick, salt and pepper hair. His piercing green eyes were enraged and he was holding a pistol in his hand.

"This way everyone! We're going to kill this little bastard!"

Principal Barnes was leading a ragtag group of faculty and students as they attempted to take the fight to Elias. I had never seen such an act of bravery. Principal Barnes was a true hero.

After the large vigilante group passed by my classroom, my surviving students and I dashed out the nearest exit to safety.

Later I found out that Elias had murdered over fifty people in the school that day.

SCHOOL SHOOTER
The Bully

I'm known as "Bad" Billy Pratt by students and teachers alike. As far as I'm concerned, I'm the biggest bully in school history and I'm proud of that fact.

I bully dozens of kids daily but my favorite target was Elias Bennings. That little dweeb was the true definition of a nerd. He got straight A's. He was into science fiction crap. He greased his hair and parted it down the middle. He wore thick, black glasses and was skinny as a rail. I mean, how could I not bully a kid like that?

I had a lot of nicknames for Elias. Nerd, geek, dork, pansy, wussy and dolt. One of my favorite things to do was run up to Elias and punch him as hard as I could in the arm. I prided myself on leaving colorful bruises. I'd make him buy me lunch. I'd make him do my homework. And of course, I always insisted that he refer to me as, sir.

I was in math class when the shooting began. None of us could figure out where it was coming from. We were afraid that if we made a mad dash for the exit doors we'd run right into the shooter, so we stayed in the classroom, which turned out to be huge mistake.

Within minutes, the door flew open and Elias stepped inside. He wasted no time in pumping the teacher full of lead and then he turned his fury toward the students.

Elias allowed most of the kids in the front of the class to leave. Then he mowed down most of the students in the middle of the room.

I knew I was a dead man. Elias was going to take great pleasure in watching bullets enter my brain. Hell, I was probably the one that drove him crazy in the first place.

I was sitting in the last seat of the row farthest from the classroom door. Elias had already released or slaughtered the rest of the class. He shot the first two kids in the row and let the next two go.

That just left me.

I didn't even bother begging for my life. I had been horrible to the kid. There was no way in the world he was going to let me live no matter what I said, so I didn't waste my breath. I clenched my teeth and braced for the blitz of bullets.

"Get out of here, Billy."

Elias motioned to the classroom door.

I sat there in shock. Was he letting me go?

"C'mon, Billy, go! Get the hell out of here!"

My eyes were wide with surprise and my jaw was practically scraping the floor. There had to be a catch. Maybe this was his way of torturing me. Elias was making me think he was going to let me go and then he'd shoot me in the back!

That's what I was thinking as I hurried through the classroom towards the door. When I reached the door, I expected to feel the impact of the bullets in my back, but I didn't. I couldn't help but look back over my shoulder before exiting. Elias was standing there, continuing to urge me on.

"Go!"

I almost wanted to thank Elias, but I was afraid he'd change his mind so I bolted down the hallway and ran into an army of teachers and students all being led by Principal Barnes. He was seething with anger and gripping a revolver in his hand. He was flanked by the elderly Woodshop teacher, Mr. Childs who was holding an axe handle. Next to him was the Home Economics teacher, Mrs. Palmer. She was brandishing a knife. They were joined by at least twenty students. There were all enraged and marching toward Elias.

I ducked behind a locker and watched on as Elias went to war with the vigilante squad.

SCHOOL SHOOTER
The Nerd

My name is Vance Norris. I'm Elias Benning's best friend. I had seen a change in Elias's behavior over the past two weeks, but I never saw this coming.

Elias was a genius. He was so smart and school assignments were too easy for him. That left him with a lot of spare time and he filled that void with his passion. Science Fiction.

He was the president of the Science Fiction club of which I was a member as well. We'd watch sci-fi movies and read sci-fi books and have intense, in-depth discussions. It was fun.

He was fun.

Elias was a good young man. He was caring, thoughtful and didn't deserve the constant bullying he suffered at the hands of "Bad" Billy Pratt. Billy picked on me too since I was a bona fide nerd as well, but it was nothing compared to the harsh treatment he gave Elias.

I expect most people will blame Elias's motivation on Billy. The bullying just got to be too much and it drove Elias crazy. But I don't believe that. I think something else was the cause.

One of Elias's main interests was UFOs and aliens. A year ago he joined a local UFO club. It was a group of people who shared that passion. They'd get together once a month. I'm not sure exactly what they did there. Elias never talked much about it, but I know the club meetings began to increase in frequency. They went from meeting once a month to twice a month to every week. And for the past two weeks, the group was meeting every single night.

It was during that two week period when I started to notice a distinct change in Elias's behavior. He became distant, like his head was somewhere else. There was something dark about the way he would stare at some of the students and teachers at school and I noticed he was slightly paranoid. He'd jump if certain people looked his way or walked toward him.

It was weird.

This part might seem insignificant, but it struck me as bizarre. Elias hated gum. He once described it as childish and would complain about how messy it was. I never saw him chew gum one time the entire time I knew him.

That is, until the past two weeks.

The past two weeks every single time I saw Elias he was chomping away on a piece of gum like a cow. I asked him what was up with that and he just said that he had a change of heart. He said this new gum was something special. He was anxious for me to try it, but said it was scarce.

The constant gum chewing coincided with the daily meetings of his UFO club and with his disturbing behavioral change.

When I saw that the school shooter was Elias, I didn't hesitate to run up to him. I knew I was risking my life, but deep down, I knew he wouldn't kill me. And I was correct.

"Why are you doing this, Elias? Why?"

Elias gave me a gentle pat on the shoulder.

"You need to get out of here. I don't want you to get hurt."

No sooner did those words leave Elias's mouth when he aimed his rifle and shot our good friend and fellow Science Fiction club nerd, Clark, in the head.

I couldn't move. I stood there frozen in terror as I watched Elias massacre our fellow classmates. I couldn't believe it when I saw him let "Bad" Billy

Pratt go. He shot our friend Clark to death, but let Billy the bully live? It didn't make sense!

That's when I saw the lynch mob led by Principal Barnes. He had fire in his eyes and was red with fury. He was leading an oddball army of students, faculty, and security guards. When several police officers showed up, Principal Barnes started barking orders at them and they fell right in line. He even commanded one of them to hand him his shotgun and they did so without hesitation.

"Elias! Today is the day you die!"

Principal Barnes opened fire on Elias as did the police and security guards. Several bullets hit Elias, but he squeezed off a massive amount of shots in return that took down more than half of the aggressive mob. His final shot hit Principal Barnes right between the eyes.

After that, it seemed Elias had run out of ammo and the remaining members of the army descended upon him like locusts. Some were shooting Elias while the others beat him with their weapons and fists.

Elias was ripped to pieces when they finished with him.

SCHOOL SHOOTER
The Shooter

When I joined the local UFO group in my town, I did so with the intention of meeting other people with similar interests.

I've always been big into science fiction, but lately had become much more passionate about science fact and finding the truth behind UFOs and alien life forms on other planets.

The first several meetings I attended consisted of getting updated on the latest UFO sightings around the world and hours of chitchatting and theorizing.

When a scientist named Dr. John Copper joined the group, my life changed.

At first most of us thought of Dr. Copper as eccentric at best and a complete loon at worst. He was convinced that a reptilian race of aliens had infiltrated our planet and walked among us. Their mission was to gradually take over the planet right under our noses.

That was the kind of story I would expect from my high school Science Fiction club, but Dr. Copper was dead serious and insisted that he would be able to prove it.

And he did.

Dr. Copper created a gooey form of gum that was infused with chemical agents that he said would wake us from our slumber and let us see the world for what it really was.

I detested chewing gum, but I was anxious to try it, for the gum would either oust Dr. Copper as a nut or prove the most significant scientific discovery in our world's history.

What I witnessed made me shiver in fear. Nearly half the people in the world were not human, but some kind of reptilian humanoid. Somehow the invaders had managed to cloak the world from their presence. Dr. Copper said it was something to do with a compound they were able to introduce into the air. To everyone else, the reptilians appeared to be normal people.

The gum wasn't convenient and it tasted like dirt. It also took several hours of constant chewing before the chemical would seep into the bloodstream enough to counter the effects of the air pollutants. Dr. Copper said he was close to finishing a liquid form of the solution that would be much easier to administer.

Once he perfected that, we could wake people up in droves.

Before Dr. Copper was able to complete the liquid solution, the reptilians discovered his creation and murdered him and destroyed all of the gum. They then showed up to the next UFO meeting and killed everyone in the group, except for me. I was the only one who managed to escape the meeting alive. But the reptoids knew who I was and they would be coming after me. It was only a matter of time before they murdered me too.

But I wasn't going down without a fight!

For the past two weeks I had been chewing the solution gum in school and observed the reptilian's comings and goings. Principal Barnes was a high ranking reptoid. Woodshop teacher Mr. Childs and the Home Economics teacher, Mrs. Palmer, were his main underlings. More than half of the student body consisted of the reptilian intruders as did the security guards.

I still had one piece of gum left in my pocket. It would be enough to allow me to see for as long as I needed to. Attacking them at the school would be the easiest way for me to take as many with me as I could.

And that's what I did.

THE SAFE UNDER THE STAIRS

I'm a recently divorced man who was in dire need of a change of scenery, so I bought a three story building in the historic district of the small, but active town of Bardstown, Kentucky. The 1st floor of the building was setup to be a business and the 2nd and 3rd floors were designed to be apartments.

I loved Bardstown and visited it quite often when my ex-wife would allow for it. She was a city girl who hated everything about small towns that I loved. It was liberating to be free from the restraints of her and the life I left behind. I was looking forward to starting over again.

The building didn't need much in the way of work. The elderly woman I bought it from had run a store there for many decades and was retiring. My plan was to rent the 1st floor to a business, rent the 2nd floor to a tenant and to live on the 3rd floor.

Without having put out any word, I had already been approached by multiple merchants and tenants who were seriously interested in the available spaces. I just needed to tidy things up a little and then I'd start the leasing process.

In the back of the building was a rear entrance that led to a large, winding stairwell. Those were the stairs that led to the 2nd and 3rd floor residences and was also the employee entrance for the 1st floor business.

There was a rather large storage space under the stairs that still had several items stored there from the previous business. It was mostly junk items that wouldn't be useful to anyone so I piled it all up and hauled it to the dumpster.

Once that area was cleared of the debris, I noticed that the storage space curved around out of sight to the back of the stairwell. I crawled back there and that's when I saw the safe.

The safe was very old. I would venture to guess it was from the 1970's at least. It was approximately 3 cubic feet around and heavy duty. This wasn't some cheap knock off brand. This was a serious safe likely meant to hold some significant assets.

The most mysterious aspect of the safe was the haggard piece of paper that had been taped to the front of it. The paper had yellowed with age, but the four words handwritten in bold letters were still very legible.

DO NOT OPEN EVER!

Technically, the safe was mine. But still, I felt the right thing to do was to contact the woman I bought the building from to see if it was hers and if there was anything inside that she wanted.

The old woman was aware of the safe under the stairs but said it had been sitting under there for so long that she had completely forgotten about it. Evidently, the safe was under the stairs when her and her husband bought the building back in the late 1950's and they heeded the warning and never attempted to open it.

A safe sitting under the stairs unopened for over 65 years? There could be gold bars in there for all I knew! My curiosity was not going to allow me to leave it be, even with the cryptic message affixed to it. If anything, that intrigued me more!

I asked around town and there was one locksmith in particular who came highly recommended. He was a short, stout man who was very open about the fact that he used to rob banks. He boasted that there wasn't a safe in the world he couldn't open.

When the locksmith crawled behind the stairs and spotted the safe in question, he was impressed. He said it was a top of the line 1930's Sentry safe.

1930's? I was shocked. This thing had been sitting under those stairs for nearly 100 years!

The man told me that if I wanted to sell the safe after I was through with it, he'd be interested in buying it as a collectible. Apparently, he didn't see many like that anymore.

I took pleasure in watching the locksmith work. He was like a surgeon as he pressed the end of a stethoscope against the face of the safe and turned the dial around and around. In less than fifteen minutes we both heard the clank of the safe door unlocking.

"That's it."

That locksmith got up and started to leave. I was rather surprised that he didn't want to see the contents of the safe.

"Don't you want to see what's inside?"

He shook his head.

"Nope. The note said not to open it. Ever. I'm going to assume there's a good reason for that. Good luck."

With that, the skilled locksmith left.

As I eyed the safe door, my heart began to accelerate and I could feel the palms of my hands begin to sweat. The moment of truth was here. There was no turning back now!

I gripped the lever of the safe and gave it a hefty tug. It budged slightly, but I was going to have to use a lot more elbow grease to get the door ajar. I pulled again, harder. It was trying to give, but seemed as though it might be stuck.

Finally, I put my foot against the wall for leverage and pulled back on the safe's door with all of my might. That did the trick. The safe door opened with a loud whoosh as if it had been vacuum sealed shut. I actually felt a rush of air blast against my face and reeled back in surprise.

I startled when the back stairwell door flung open. I quickly got up and looked around. There was nobody outside or in the stairwell. I didn't see a soul. And the night was still. There wasn't any kind of wind gusts or breeze to contribute to the door's sudden opening. I was at a loss.

I brushed that happening aside and focused on the safe. It was time to find out what was in it! I withdrew a small penlight from my shirt pocket, pulled the safe door all the way opened and shined it inside.

I was hoping for gold bullion, jewelry, cash or coins. But none of those things were inside. As a matter of fact there was only one thing within the safe. It was a lock of black human hair tied together with a rubber band. There was no indication as to who the hair belonged to or why it was there.

And just like that, the mystery surrounding what was inside the safe had been solved.

But I wasn't satisfied.

The following day I did some serious research on the building's history. According to what I found, the man who owned the building in the 1930's rented the commercial portion to a young woman who used it to peddle potions and incantations. In the late 1930's the woman was arrested for teaching classes on how to perform live sacrifices.

Unfortunately, that was all I was able to find out. The mystery of the lock of hair and the cryptic note on the safe would go unsolved.

That night I slept heavy and had the most vivid of dreams. I dreamt of an attractive young woman with long, raven hair. She was dressed in black and donned an unusual, pointed hat. The woman was stirring boiling liquid in a cast iron caldron as she chanted.

Across from the woman was a naked man. He was bound by rope and begging for his life. The woman flashed a sadistic grin his way and spoke with an airy voice.

"You have rejected my spells and potions and refuse to be mine. Now, you will suffer the consequences."

The woman proceeded to clip a lock of black hair from the man's head. She then bound the hair with a rubber band as she closed her eyes and chanted in an unknown language. Suddenly, her dark eyes snapped open and she snarled at the man.

"Your soul will be trapped!"

I heard a heavy, metallic pound followed by silence and blackness.

For the longest time I heard nothing but shallow breaths that eventually transitioned into subtle whimpering.

I could feel myself wincing in my sleep as a blinding light illuminated my face and suddenly I felt myself floating in the air like a dried leaf tumbling from the branch of a mighty tree.

Once the brightness began to fade, I found myself standing in the stairwell staring at the man who I had seen bound by rope. He was wearing a brown, tweed 3-piece suit with a white shirt, blue tie and tan fedora. He shook my hand and smiled as he spoke.

"Thank you."

I woke up in a cold sweat, panting to catch my breath. I felt exhausted and my muscles ached. I had no energy and collapsed back onto the bed and blacked out before waking up the next morning fully rested.

Was that just an intense dream? Or did I truly free a man's trapped soul? I'll never know for sure, but every now and then when I'm in the stairwell of that building, I can feel an overwhelming sense of gratitude lingering in the air.

THE BIZARRE RESTAURANT

I had only lived in Chicago for a few months. I moved from rural Tennessee for a job opportunity and quite frankly, I was missing the country.

I did however meet a lot of nice people and had gone out on dates with a few different girls. That was the plan for the night in question as well.

Robin was a secretary at the office complex I worked. I saw her every day on the way in and out of work. Polite smiles accompanying our hellos and goodbyes evolved into friendly chit chat which eventually transitioned to legitimate conversations. I felt we had progressed to the point where a date might be in order so I asked and she accepted.

In an attempt to make the first date memorable, I made reservations at one of the city's most respected fine dining establishments. Robin lived in the suburbs of the city and rather than have me pick her up, she decided we should just meet at the restaurant.

The reservation was for 7:30pm. I was standing outside the restaurant staring at my watch which boldly stated the time of 7:45pm, when my phone rang. It was Robin. She was extremely apologetic as she explained that she was stricken with a sudden bout of nausea and would not be able to make our date. She suggested that we postpone until the following weekend, if I was still interested. Of course I was, so I told her that would be great.

The problem was, I was starving! I needed food and fast. I wasn't going to eat at the fine dining establishment alone, so I decided pizza would be a nice consolation prize.

One thing I quickly learned about Chicago was that when it came to pizza, you couldn't go wrong, so rather than spend time scrolling through my phone searching for the nearest pizzeria, I decided to take a stroll down the block and the first pizza place I saw would be the winner.

Less than a block away a flickering pizza sign was beckoning to me and I picked up my pace. I was so focused on the restaurant that I didn't even notice the small accumulation of people stopped on the sidewalk in front of me. I nearly rammed into the back of a little old lady who was gawking down at the unfortunate sight before us.

An elegant woman in her late 60's wearing a sparkling evening gown was lying on her back. She appeared to be passed out. A panicked man in a tuxedo and long coat was on his knees gently slapping both sides of the woman's face in an attempt to revive her. There was a buzz of chatter and I heard someone ask him what happened.

"I don't know, she said she felt dizzy and just collapsed!"

An ambulance zoomed onto the scene before I could offer any assistance, not that my first-aid ignorant abilities would have been any help anyway.

The EMT's were quick to examine the woman, get her on a gurney and load her into the ambulance. As the tuxedoed man began stepping into the back of the ambulance with her, he reached into his coat pocket and pulled out his cellphone. In doing so, a large, thick piece of white paper fell from his pocket and floated to the ground.

"Hey, you dropped something!"

I rushed toward the ambulance to retrieve the paper for the man, but the ambulance doors shut and the vehicle sped away before I could reach it.

I watched the ambulance race away into the distance before I bent down and picked up the paper that fell from the man's pocket.

The paper was very thick and as I examined it, I recognized it as a fancy, embroidered invitation. At the top of the card in gold, embossed, cursive font was the name of a restaurant. Restaurant Bizarre.

Underneath the title, the invitation read as follows: Congratulations. This ticket is good for one admission to the most coveted exclusive, restaurant in the city. Entry is allowed via invitation only.

My intrigue coupled with my rumbling stomach made my decision a no-brainer. I was going to eat at Restaurant Bizarre.

I followed the directions on the back of the invitation to a nondescript building with a facade that was painted black. The large door in the center of the building was framed with long, thin white lights. A man in his later 30's dressed in a tailor-made suit stood outside the door. He recognized my confusion as I gazed about for some kind of signage.

"May I help you sir?"

I held up the invitation.

"I have this admission ticket…"

Before I could finish my sentence, the man smiled and opened the door.

"Welcome to Restaurant Bizarre."

I entered and found myself alone in a small lobby that was sparkling with cleanliness. The floor and ceilings were white. The walls were black. A marble counter was positioned near the rear of the room.

After waiting a brief moment a woman dressed in a tight, yet sophisticated dress stepped behind the counter. Her auburn hair was tied back in a tight bun and her cat-like, emerald eyes sparkled as she spoke to me.

"May I have your admission ticket, please?"

I handed her the invitation. She studied it briefly before holding it under a small black-light device. Once satisfied she looked up and nodded.

"Congratulations. Your ticket has been deemed authentic."

The woman stared at me as if waiting for some type of response. After a few seconds of awkward silence, I spoke up.

"Uh. Great. Thanks."

The woman gave me a polite nod before speaking again.

"You can place your order with me, sir."

"Uh, okay. Can I have a menu?"

The woman stared at me indifferently as if I said something that offended her.

"Wait here for the maître d."

After a brief wait, a petite man with slicked black hair and a toothbrush mustache entered the room. He wore a white dress shirt with a black tie and vest.

"I understand you requested a menu. Menus are not available at Restaurant Bizarre. You have your choice of the house traditional or the house special. Both dishes are served with roasted beet salad, honey-crisp apples, pumpernickel, almonds and blue cheese."

"What do the house traditional and the house special consist of?"

The maître d closed his eyes as he allowed a short, pompous chuckle to escape from his lips.

"At Restaurant Bizarre, choices are limited and a certain amount of risk and trust are required. It's part of the experience which makes us who we are."

It was a little…well, bizarre, but I was willing to play along. I just wanted some food and fast.

"What do you recommend?"

The maître d did not hesitate.

"The house special tonight is exquisite."

I nodded.

"Very well."

The maître d led me down a blackened corridor and opened a door to a small room that housed a solid white table and chair. A single rose placed delicately within a thin, clear vase was the lone centerpiece.

The maître d pulled my chair out for me. Once I was seated he gave me a rather odd choice.

"Would you prefer your salad to be served in a plate or a bowl?"

I shrugged.

"A plate would be fine."

"And would you rather a fork or a spoon to eat your salad with? I recommend a fork."

He was dead serious. I simply nodded and went with his daring recommendation of a fork.

It hadn't been but two minutes before my roasted beet salad arrived. The portion was on the dainty side but what it lacked in quantity, it made up for with quality. Each bite was an explosion of flavor. I was truly saddened when I finished the last bite. But if the salad was any indication of what I was in store for with the main course, I was in for something special!

After my table was cleared the maître d made another appearance.

"Your dinner will be ready shortly. Would you prefer to be fed by a male or female?"

"Fed?"

"Ah yes, the house special is fed to you. There is no other way. Your only choice is a male or female feeder."

I muttered under my breath.

"Restaurant Bizarre, indeed."

"Excuse me sir?"

I shook my head and grinned.

"A female feeder would be preferred."

The maître d bowed his head and exited the room.

What the hell kind of place was this? I barely finished my thought when my feeder entered the room. She was a woman in her late 40's void of makeup and dressed in a plain black dress. Her raven hair was tied back with a white ribbon. Her voice was soft and timid.

"My name is Greta. I will be your feeder. I have been informed that your house special is ready for consumption."

Greta held up a large black cloth that she began folding.

"It is time for you to be blindfolded."

"Blindfolded?"

"Correct. It is part of the experience here at Restaurant Bizarre. We believe the visual vacancy exemplifies your sense of taste."

At that point I just wanted to eat, so I gave no objections as she blindfolded me and the room became black.

As she finished tying the blindfold, I heard the door to the room open and a sudden sharp, rich peppery aroma filled the air. I could feel hot, scented steam gliding over my face as the house special was placed before me. Before the feeder commenced with her duties, she gave me a stern warning.

"Under no circumstances are you to take off your blindfold. When the time comes, I will remove it for you. Do you understand?"

"Yes."

"Please open your mouth."

I did as was instructed and something large and round was placed in my mouth. It was firm and had the texture of a large olive, but its flavor was bold and savory. The feeder instructed me to bite down. When I did, a spurt of tangy juice erupted in my mouth.

Once I was finished with…whatever the hell that was, I was treated to multiple bites of some kind of spiced meat. The exterior was light and crisp, but the center was incredibly tender and melted like hot butter in my mouth. The seasoning overwhelmed me, yet it was perfect. A rich pepper coating gave way to a nut and honey glaze. It felt like a main course followed by a scrumptious dessert with every bite.

I was filling up fast had no complaints with the feeder moving on to the next food item. This was an unusual cut of meat. There was an initial sponginess to the tough texture but as I bit down, a smoky sweet and sour lemon sauce gushed from the center. It was unfamiliar, but delicious!

Next I was treated to something extremely crispy that flaked apart in my mouth. As I crunched away, my taste buds were treated to the delightful pairing of acidic citrus and savory cured meat.

I never intended to remove the blindfold. I had an itch on the back of my head, directly under it. As I scratched away, I inadvertently loosened the blindfold and it drooped down to my mouth revealing the house special in front of me.

A roasted one-eyed human head was staring up at me. I assume the other eye was the first thing I ate. The strips of missing flesh from each cheek were likely the second course. Half a tongue hanging out of the mouth and only one ear on the head told me what the other two portions I had were.

I let out a groan of disgust and as I stood up my feeder started shouting.

"Blindfold! Blindfold!"

Within seconds multiple brawny men in black suits rushed into the room and shoved me against the wall. As they held me, the maître d entered the room with a disappointed expression.

"You were told not to remove the blindfold, yes?"

"It was an accident!"

"That makes no difference. I'm sure you can understand why we cannot let you go."

Before I could beg and plead for my life, I was gagged. When a man dressed in a chef's outfit entered the room and informed everyone that they were all out of the house special, the maître d looked back at me, held up a butcher knife and grinned.

"I believe we have one more."

BARREN WORLD
The Woman

I'm a 41 year old woman, which makes me one of the youngest people in the entire world.

Forty years ago, every female on the planet became barren.

Nobody knows why.

The only time I've ever seen a human baby was when I was a baby myself and those memories are so distant they don't seem real.

My happiest moments are watching videos and movies with babies. Or thumbing through old magazines and seeing ads that depict families with children. It must have been wonderful. But I can only imagine.

Without question there is a void in my life knowing I can never have kids. I'll never have one. I'll never hold one. I'll never experience one in any way.

The world is a strange place. It's as though when the female of our species went barren so did the spirit. Knowing the end of the species is mere decades away and that there is nothing anyone can do about it is deflating. Ambition, energy, enthusiasm…those are things most people in our world do not possess.

It's a sad world. Life is sluggish, depressing and uninspired.

Over the barrenness decades, a form of devolution has taken place within the species. For women, a sense of purpose has vanished. And men seem to have been emasculated.

But still, we live our lives as drab as they are as we unwillingly march toward the extinction of our species.

The world has become a dangerous place. As more and more people stop caring about themselves they also stop caring about others. Morality within our species is evaporating. Thus I carry a gun and a knife with me everywhere I go. I've had to use both on more than one occasion to save my life.

I work at a hospital as a nurse. I'm part of the minority that still enjoys caring for other people. Though most of the people I help are miserable and dejected, I try to keep a smile on my face. Most days it is ineffective, but occasionally it is infectious. I live for those days. To see others happy, smiling…hopeful.

I had worked a double shift and was exhausted. The parking lot of the hospital was well lit and usually safe. That fact combined with my fatigue caused my defenses to be down.

I never saw him coming.

I felt someone grab me from behind, roughly pulling me against their body. Before I had time to reach into my purse for my gun, a rag was slapped over my face. The strong chemical smell was overwhelming and I passed out.

I only have a couple of memories after that and they are incredibly foggy, so I'm not sure how accurate they are.

I remember waking up on a bed. I felt paralyzed. I couldn't move a muscle. The room I was in looked like a medical lab of some sort. I remember seeing shelving units with various metal trays, test tubes and syringes. I believe there was a tray next to me that had a scalpel, forceps and a speculum. After that I remember someone lying on top of me, moving in a rhythmic pattern.

I woke up in a dirty alley. My lower abdomen was throbbing in pain and I was certain that I had been sexually violated.

BARREN WORLD
The Man

Aliens have invaded earth.

When I was a kid I always imagined such an event to consist of massive flying saucers shooting laser beams and decimating the cities. Perhaps ground troops of grotesque beasts would blast away at the survivors until the planet was conquered.

The truth is much less eventful, yet much more impactful.

They've rendered our species sterile. Now all they have to do is be patient. In fifty to sixty years humans will be extinct and they can simply move in with minimal effort.

But unlike most of my fellow species, I'm not going down without a fight!

I've spent my entire adult life researching how the sterilization took place. I became a gynecologist so that I would be an expert in the female anatomy. I made a decision to do anything it took to discover what had happened. No matter how despicable my actions may need to be.

I had studied enough living subjects. The time had come for something more crucial. I began kidnapping woman and mutilating them. I carved them up like a modern day Jack the Ripper. Not because I was some psychopathic missing link, but rather in an effort to save the species. If I was going to find out how they managed to sterilize women, I needed to study every millimeter of them.

I must have butchered over a hundred women, but after scrutinizing every portion of the female body under a powerful microscope, I found it.

A nanobot.

This microscopic alien robot guards the female egg and destroys any sperm that approaches. I'm not entirely sure how the aliens introduced the robot, but I would venture to guess the source to most likely be drinking water.

I killed another hundred women as I tried to perfect the removal of the nanobot. While it was not easy, I'm now an expert at it.

I could teach what I learned to others and we could remove the nanobots from every fertile woman in the world and also the inevitable offspring they will produce.

I have saved the human species.

However, slaughtering all of those women has done something to me. Without question it has numbed my conscience and warped my mind. Recognizing this fact makes me no less crazy and my insanity now drives me.

Why should I teach my skill to others? Why share the credit? Why should I let others fertilize the women? That honor should be all mine!

I spend my nights stalking women, waiting for the perfect moment and then I subdue them, sedate them and impregnate them. This is my daily routine.

Some may call me a murderer and a rapist. They would not be wrong. But in my sick, demented mind...I'm also a hero. More than that, I am the new Adam and every woman in the world is *my* Eve!

MY ROOMMATE

I went to college out of state and was excited to begin the next chapter in my life. I was hoping to get to my dorm room early in the day, but hadn't accounted for traffic and by the time I arrived it was late afternoon.

When I entered my dorm room, I was greeted by my new roommate, Nancy. She had cute short brown hair with subtle pink highlights, but the most unique aspect of Nancy was that she had two different colored eyes. One was brown and one was dark green.

I explained to her that I live out of state and ran into traffic along the way or I would have gotten there earlier.

"Don't worry about it. I live out of state too. I took some back roads to avoid traffic. I hope you don't mind that I took the bed on the right side of the room."

I didn't care at all. The room was tiny and the beds were identical. Nancy then pointed to the closet located at the foot of her bed.

"All I ask is that you don't go into my closet. It's a mess. I just threw all my stuff in there. It's going to take me a few days to organize."

I told her she had nothing to worry about. I was the private type and would never consider rummaging through other people's things.

Nancy seemed sweet. We talked for hours as I unpacked and got my side of the room in order. I told her where I was from and all about my family. Nancy said she was an only child and expressed that she always wanted a sibling. She was hoping that we could eventually be like sisters.

That night I turned in early. I was exhausted from the drive and the excitement of the day. I woke up at 1:00am. When I opened my eyes, I saw Nancy sitting on the edge of her bed, watching me. She felt the need to explain herself.

"I have a difficult time sleeping in new places. It'll pass. Don't worry about me. Go back to sleep."

I did so, but two hours later, my full bladder woke me up. When I got up to use the bathroom, I saw Nancy lying on her bed. She was awake, resting her head in her hand and staring directly at me.

"Hi roomie."

I smiled as best as I could for still being half asleep. After using the bathroom, I crawled back in bed. When I glanced in Nancy's direction, I caught her looking at me again. She didn't even pretend that she wasn't. She just kept gawking at me. I was too tired to care much and fell back to sleep.

The next morning I woke up and Nancy wasn't in the room. I'm the kind of person who is never fully awake until they have a shower, so I immediately went to the bathroom, shut the door behind me and got into the shower.

While in the midst of my invigorating shower, I heard a light tap on the bathroom door. This was followed by the creak of the door opening and Nancy's voice.

"Do you mind if I come in for a minute? I have to get something. I promise I won't look."

Again, I'm the private type and not keen on people entering the bathroom while I'm in there, but I wasn't going to risk coming off rude this early in a new relationship. Nancy would understand my preferences more once we got to know each other better.

"Okay. That's fine."

I heard her moving around in the bathroom for a couple of minutes, followed by the door closing after she left. Even so, I felt compelled to peek out through the shower curtain to make sure she wasn't still in the bathroom before I stepped out of the shower.

Nancy was not in the dorm room when I exited the bathroom in my robe. I had just finished getting dressed when there was a knock at the dorm room door. When I opened the door, a woman in her early 40's was standing there. She had long, fine blonde hair and bright blue eyes. She held a look of concern on her face.

"Is Nancy here?"

"She just stepped out. Can I help you?"

"I'm Nancy's mom."

"Oh, nice to meet you! Come on in."

Nancy's mom was apologetic for the intrusion but explained that she was worried about her daughter.

"Nancy promised to call me every night before she went to bed and she didn't call last night. I tried her phone several times this morning, but she never answered so I thought I'd stop by real quick and check on her."

"I can assure you she's fine. She was just here a few minutes ago."

I could see the relief in the woman's face upon hearing that her daughter was okay, but something about her statement confused me.

"Don't you live out of state? That must have been a long drive for you."

She cocked her head slightly before speaking.

"Out of state? No. We live just fifteen minutes away. Anyhow, I don't want to come across as a meddlesome mother so I'll be on my way, but can you ask Nancy to call me? Her father, brother and I want to have dinner with her tonight."

"Of course I will. It was nice to meet you."

I found myself bewildered yet again. Nancy's mother mentioned a brother. But Nancy had told me she was an only child. Was she some kind of pathological liar?

It was about an hour later when Nancy returned. She was beaming.

"Did you know they have a miniature golf course just off of campus? I love miniature golf. What do you say we play a round and then maybe have dinner and then go see a movie?"

"Nancy, your mother was just here."

Nancy's demeanor instantly changed. Her smile dropped into a frown. Her eyes filled with nervousness and began darting around the room.

"She was?"

"Yes. She said she lived just fifteen minutes from here. But you told me you lived out of state."

Nancy began pacing back and forth and pulling at her short hair.

"Dammit! Why can't she just leave me alone?"

"Are you okay, Nancy?"

She snapped at me.

"No! I'm not okay."

Once she realized that her tone was aggressive, she produced a remorseful smile and took in a deep breath.

"I'm sorry. I should have told you the truth. I just…I *wish* I lived farther away from here. That's why I said that."

Tears began rolling down Nancy's cheeks and she rushed over and sat next to me on the bed. She sat very close, wrapped her arms around me and buried her head in my chest as she sobbed.

I tried to be sympathetic. I stroked the back of her short hair as I spoke.

"Don't cry, Nancy. It's going to be okay. You're starting a new life now and whatever happened before is the past. Try to look forward to the future."

My compassion seemed to calm Nancy down. Her sobbing trailed off and she began sniffing.

"Thanks for being here for me. I love you so much."

I had known Nancy for less than twenty four hours so that was a bit of an extreme statement in my opinion and Nancy seemed to recognize that as well.

"Uh…I mean…just thank you for being here for me."

I smiled and politely broke her tight hug by standing up.

"It's okay, Nancy. Oh, but your mom did say she wanted you to call her. She wants you to go out to dinner with her and your father tonight. And your brother. Didn't you say you were an only child?"

This sent Nancy into a rage. She stood up and started pacing around the room like a caged tiger as she yelled.

"That bitch! Why did she have to come here? Why can't she leave me alone? I could just kill her!"

Nancy stormed out of the room and slammed the door shut.

That was weird. Clearly Nancy had some deep seeded emotional issues. It left me feeling like *I* needed to be comforted, so I picked up my phone to dial my dad.

When I opened my phone, I noticed that it was open to the photo gallery page. And the first picture I saw was of me…sleeping.

That's when I realized that it wasn't *my* phone I was holding, it was Nancy's phone. She left it on my bed when she bolted out of the room and I picked it up thinking it was mine.

I scrolled through the recent pictures on Nancy's phone. They were all of me. There were multiple shots of me sleeping in my bed the previous night and two blurry images of me in the shower.

I was horrified. I was considering whether I should confront her or report her when there was another knock on the door. I feared it was Nancy. I was relieved when it wasn't.

Standing at the door were two men from the college administrator's office and Nancy's mother. They explained that Nancy had not shown up for any of her morning classes or to pick up her ID badge.

When they held up the ID badge, my blood ran cold. The name on the badge was Nancy Newman. The picture was of a fair skinned, light blonde girl with bright blue eyes.

My mouth was dry. I had to lick my lips a few times before I could speak.

"That's…I've never seen that girl before. That's not the Nancy who claimed to be my roommate."

The school officials were alarmed by my words and immediately began looking through Nancy's side of the room. When they opened the closet at the foot of Nancy's bed, the dead body of the real Nancy fell out.

The official investigation concluded that the imposter had arrived early the previous morning to the dorm room. No one knows why she killed the real Nancy and tried to impersonate her.

The phone that had been used to take the creepy pictures of me was the real Nancy's phone. There was nothing else on it to help them find the imposter Nancy.

They had no idea who the imposter was or where she went.

Obviously, I didn't feel comfortable at that college anymore and I left. I went back home and worked a part-time job for a few months before enrolling the following semester at a college close to home.

The scariest thing about it all is the fact that the crazy woman posing as my roommate knew my name and where I was from.

It wouldn't be difficult for her to find me if she wanted to.

THE WRONG BUS

I'm a big burly guy. I was an offensive tackle on my college football team so it may surprise some people to know that I have a low threshold for pain. But it's true.

When I got a cavity in one of my back molars that was aching daily, I told the dentist I just wanted it yanked so the pain would go away. Sure I'd have to deal with the post pulling pain, but that would subside after a few days, so that was the choice I made.

I insisted that the dentist give me nitrous oxide before injecting me with Novocain to numb my mouth. The injection still stung like a bitch, but by the time he was finished pulling my tooth I felt like I was floating and didn't feel a thing.

The dentist prescribed me some painkillers which I filled at a pharmacy just a few doors down from his office. I popped double the recommended dosage in my mouth after checking out.

I knew ahead of time that I would be in no shape to drive after the procedure, so I had made a point to take a bus to the dentist's office. Lucky for me, the bus station was just a few blocks away.

The combination of nitrous oxide and too many painkillers had me walking in a daze to the bus station. I was surprised I even made it. Everyone around me seemed to be moving in slow motion and I think I was walking in circles for a little while, but eventually I found myself on a bus. There was no bus driver in sight, which gave me pause, but then I noticed six or seven other people scattered around the bus, so I figured it was safe to board.

I grabbed a seat at the rear of the bus and rested my head against the window. The cool glass felt good against my skin. I was groggy. Each blink of my heavy eyelids seemed to take five seconds.

As I stared out the window I saw the bus driver. He was a hefty man wearing a drab gray uniform. The name of the bus company was stenciled on his sleeve. I noticed he was chatting to a police officer or maybe it was a security guard. I squinted as I tried to make out the writing on his arm patch. I was pretty sure it said McCracken Insane Asylum. Then I fell asleep.

I woke up when the bus hit a massive pothole that shook me to my core. I rubbed my dry eyes and shook my head slightly to clear the cobwebs from my brain. While I was still feeling the effects from the pain medication, it had worn off enough that I was much more aware of my unusual surroundings.

The first thing that struck me as odd was that the bus was driving down a neglected gravel road through the middle of a thick, dark forest. This didn't make sense. There was no forest anywhere near my bus stop. I lived in the middle of a city.

I rubbed my eyes some more and turned my focus to the other passengers on the bus. They were all male. They appeared groggy with their heads tilted down. Their limp bodies shook around with each bump the bus hit.

Had I gotten on the wrong bus?

I tried to rise from my seat and call out to the bus driver, but the combination of the bumpy road and my weakened state caused me to fall right back down into my seat. As I steadied myself, I noticed a shift in the environment outside. The forest had given way to a clearing and just up ahead in the distance I could see a small, old ghost town.

As the bus got closer to the town, I noticed that there was a ten foot tall chain link fence topped with razor wire, encircling the town. I shook my head a few more times to make sure I wasn't hallucinating. The bus's headlights confirmed the visual.

When the bus came to a halt outside of the fence, I watched on as the bus driver got out of the vehicle, opened the main gate and then returned. He then proceeded to drive the bus into the middle of the town before stopping again.

We were in a legitimate ghost town. It was abandoned, weathered and worn. It consisted of a dozen different buildings. It had the look of a late 1880's old west town. I even spotted a saloon with swinging doors. The only thing missing were some tumbleweeds blowing across the street.

I startled when the bus driver stood up, faced the passengers and held up a cattle prod in a threatening manner.

"Okay you lowlifes, get the hell off my bus!"

The other passengers looked up sluggishly as if trying to ascertain what the bus driver was trying to convey. The bus driver's next move left no doubt.

"Get out! Now!"

The bus driver began pressing the intimidating end of the cattle prod against the passenger's bodies. The ones he touched let out screams of pain and quickly found their balance as they stood up and rushed off the bus. It was then that I realized that all of the other passengers on the bus were handcuffed and were dressed in white jumpsuits that had a McCracken Insane Asylum logo stenciled on the back.

After the final passenger was off, the bus driver turned his head in my direction and locked eyes with me. Anger took over his expression.

"I said get off the bus!"

As the enraged bus driver bolted down the aisle toward me, I stood up and held out my hands.

"No! You don't understand…"

The bus driver was perplexed by my lack of handcuffs.

"How the hell did you get out of your cuffs? Get over here!"

The bus driver grabbed me by the back of my neck and began shoving me down the aisle toward the bus entrance. I pleaded my case as he manhandled me.

"I got on the wrong bus! I thought this was the bus that went to Jefferson and 5th street!"

As we reached the bus doors, the bus driver paused when he noticed that I was dressed in street clothes.

He looked me up and down and slowly came to a realization.

"You're not kidding. You really did get on the wrong bus, didn't you?"

I didn't have a chance to answer when I heard the horrendous aggressive howl of something wild. The roar was quickly accompanied by growls and snarls. Within seconds, my ears were ringing with the savage sounds of monsters. Dozens of them.

Zombies.

They were lumbering out of the buildings of the ghostly town making their way for the handcuffed passengers.

It was obvious that the passengers had been heavily drugged, but they were still aware of the impending doom and attempted to run away. They were too lethargic to outrun the zombies who swarmed the passengers and began ripping them apart.

My mouth was agape as I watched on in horror.

"This is where we take dangerous lunatics when they attack the staff."

I turned and looked at the bus driver who seemed to be enjoying the explanation.

"You've got bad luck buddy. I always pick the crazies up at the asylum. Tonight the bus started breaking down. I had to pull over at the bus station and swap vehicles. You must have gotten on when I wasn't looking."

He shrugged.

"I wish I could take you back, but I'm afraid you've seen too much."

The bus driver maintained a sadistic grin as he held up the cattle prod.

I knew if he touched me with that thing, I would fall backwards out of the bus and would be a meal for the zombies. I'm not sure if it was the fear of the electric shock or the fear of being torn apart, but I knew an intolerable amount of pain was in my future if I didn't act fast.

It was obvious that the bus driver wasn't expecting me to fight back for he was shocked when I grabbed the base of the cattle prod. He gripped it tighter as he tried to pull it away from me and that was his mistake. I yanked on the cattle prod which caused him to stumble down the stairs past me and out the door.

I immediately jumped in the driver's seat and closed the bus door. The driver began shouting and pounding on the glass as he tried to get back in. The ruckus he made immediately drew the zombie's attention and they swarmed him like starving sharks.

I quickly drove the bus out of there. I stopped and refastened the gate to make sure the zombies didn't escape and then drove back to the city. I parked the bus on a street corner a few blocks from my apartment and then walked home.

I slept like the dead. It was nearly 24 hours later when I woke up. My mouth was throbbing in pain from my extracted tooth, but my mind was no longer clouded from all the pain medicine.

The crazy events that took place the previous day seemed like nothing more than a vivid nightmare. And I like to think that in reality that's all it was, just a pain medication induced, realistic nightmare.

But I know it wasn't.

THE OCTOBER 13TH HOUSE
The Owners

The house was brand new. Nobody had ever lived there. We didn't really care why someone would build such a beautiful two-story Cape Cod only to turn around and sell it. They must have had their reasons and their loss was our gain.

We loved the neighborhood. It was sparsely populated with plenty of room between houses. The distance from my husband's workplace was no more than a fifteen minute drive and my 8 year old son's school was considered one of the best in the county.

We moved into the house on May 12th.

It was a beautiful, lively spring day. I was planting some bushes in the front yard when a spindly, elderly man wearing a stained white shirt and a black vest rode by on his bicycle. He stopped at the front of the driveway, removed his soiled porkpie hat and wiped the sweat from his brow.

"That plot of land your house sits on is cursed, you know. It has a death curse."

I didn't even have a chance to respond before the old man pedaled away. Apparently I met the town crazy.

When our nearest neighbors came over with a plate of cookies that night to welcome us to the neighborhood, I mentioned the strange man on the bicycle. They explained he was a kooky old fool who lived a couple miles away. They insisted that while he was strange, he was harmless. I asked if they had any idea why he would think the land was cursed. The wife spoke up.

"I think his imagination just started to run wild after those deaths."

"Deaths?"

"Oh yes. All of the original contractors died while building your house. They all died on the same day. October 13th. It was so unusual. What was it honey, a lightning strike?"

The husband nodded.

"I believe so. Which makes the most logical sense. None of crew members who took over died or had any mishaps as you would expect from a supposed death curse."

While my neighbors brushed aside the tragic incident, I was left with a haunting feeling and decided to do a little research.

I contacted the gentleman we bought the house from and inquired as to why he decided to sell the house. At first he was vague and simply stated he had a change of heart, but he changed his tune when I asked him a direct question.

"Did it have anything to do with those men dying when building the house?"

He shrugged.

"It was more about the *day* they all died on. October 13th. Call me superstitious, but that seemed like a bad omen."

"So that's why you sold the house?"

"That's what gave me initial pause. But I loved that neighborhood. I loved the house. I wasn't going to give it all up if I wasn't sure."

"Sure about what?"

"That it had a death curse."

I smiled.

"Sounds like you met the crazy old man on the bike too."

He nodded.

"Yes. I thought he was a loon at first too. Then I hired a private detective who dug up some history that I simply couldn't ignore."

"What kind of history?"

"The land your house sits on was a Creek Indian burial ground. That's another bad omen."

I found myself nodding in agreement as he continued.

"I wasn't the first person to build a house on that land. In 1911, a man built a log cabin in the exact spot your house sits now. On October 13th of that year, a tornado leveled the cabin killing the man and his wife."

The man leaned forward.

"And that's just the tip of the iceberg. In the 1930's archeologists began excavating the burial ground. Three of them died of heart attacks while digging. The date of their deaths was October 13th. In the

1950's kids used to use that area as a drag strip. There were some crashes. And one death. On October 13th."

I couldn't believe what he was saying.

"This is all verified?"

He chuckled.

"I was skeptical myself, but it all checks out. For a couple years in the 1960's your land was used as the local lover's lane. On October 13th, 1965 a young man and his girlfriend were shot to death. The following year on October 13th two teenagers committed suicide in the same spot. They closed it off at that point. I can go on."

I was captivated and terrified. I didn't want to hear anymore but I had to.

"Please do."

"October 13th 1975, loggers clearing the land used that spot to set fire to the chopped trees. They all burned to death. October 13th 1985 when leveling the ground, a man fell from his bulldozer and was crushed to death. October 13th, 1991 a woman drowned in the pond in your back yard. October 13th, 1998 a boy was practicing archery and fell onto his arrow which went through his eye and punctured his brain, killing him instantly. October 13th, 2004 two women camping on the land were attacked and killed by a black bear. October 13th, 2008…"

That's when I stopped him. I had heard enough. I was convinced. And I didn't take it all at face value either. I checked into it and it was true. It was all true.

I had absolutely no doubt in my mind that if we still lived in that house on October 13th we would all die.

We sold the house on July 10th.

THE OCTOBER 13th HOUSE
The Buyer

I was positive my house was haunted. The previous owner was an old man who died in the bedroom. His wife had died ten years earlier in the same room. Legend has it that the old man had poisoned her, but there was no evidence and he was never brought up on charges.

I'm a single 39 year old woman with no prospects. I had lived alone in the house for six months and from day one I began experiencing paranormal activity.

I regularly heard pounding noises coming from the basement. I recorded the noises and posted it on social media. A lot of people suspected it may be a loose pipe banging against the wall, but I think it was a ghost.

My back door closed all by itself a few different times. I even caught it on video and posted it to the web to see what people thought. Many concluded that it was caused by a draft. But I think it was more likely caused by the spirit of the previous owner.

Often when I would sit in the living room with the TV off, I could hear the house making all kinds of strange sounds including scratching coming from behind the walls. I was able to capture this paranormal activity on my phone and posted it to social media as proof. Skeptics assumed there was a mouse behind the wall, but I think it was the ghost of the woman the man murdered, trapped in the house, trying to get out!

I was scared day and night. I had a difficult time sleeping due to all of the strange, ghostly bumps and creaks I constantly heard. I was fearful for my safety and decided to sell the house.

Fortunately, I didn't have any trouble selling it and I was determined to makes sure my next house would be ghost free.

I targeted brand new houses or homes that only had one previous owner. I would only consider the homes with previous owners if none of them had died while living there.

Eventually, I found a house that was perfect. It was a two-story Cape Cod that was less than a year old. A husband, wife and their only child lived there. According to them there was nothing wrong with the house, they simply had a change of heart.

I remember the lady of the house chuckling when I asked them if the house was haunted. When she realized I was dead serious, she made it perfectly clear that they had never experienced any paranormal activity in the home whatsoever.

I made a bid slightly over the asking price, assuming that would get me the house easily. However, it appeared I wasn't the only interested party and a bidding war ensued. Eventually, I did get the house, but I had to pay eight thousand dollars more than I originally intended to. But I loved the house. It was worth it!

I moved in on July 27th.

The neighborhood was spread out and quiet. There was a large pond in the backyard. I spent most evenings sitting on the back porch, sipping on a glass of lemonade, listening to the frogs croak, insects buzz and birds chirp. I had found peace and I was genuinely happy.

And then I heard the knocking. It started approximately one month after I had moved in.

The first time was when I was in the kitchen cooking dinner. It sounded like someone knocking on a door, but it was faint and muffled. I determined that the knocking was coming from the front of the house. I walked into the living room, but the sound had stopped. I knew the house couldn't be haunted, so I brushed it off as a probable sound outside.

A few nights later I was awakened by the same knocking sound. It was steady and repeated every two seconds. Again, it wasn't someone knocking on any of my doors. The sound was too muted for that. But still, I went downstairs and opened the front door anyway. There was nobody there and again, the knocking had stopped.

The knocking gradually became more frequent and within a week, it was occurring every single day. Usually late at night. It always emanated from the front of the house and always stopped before I could hone in on it.

I put a digital recorder in the living room and captured the sound. I posted it on social media, but nobody was impressed. They said it could be anything.

I invited friends over in hopes that they would hear the knocking and help me figure out what it was, but it never happened when anyone else was there which made me feel a little bit crazy.

It was the middle of the week when the knocking woke me up at 2:00am. It was a dark, stormy night. Rain was pelting the metal roof of the house and the raging wind outside was whistling.

I followed the knocking to the living room. Every other time I'd get close to the knocking sound, it would stop, but on this night it continued. It was the same, faint, hollow, slow rhythmic knocking and I followed it to the middle of the living room.

It was coming from under the floor.

The hair on the back of my neck was standing on end. I was chilled with goosebumps. I could hear my teeth chattering in fear. My instinct was to run, but I found myself bending down and placing my ear against the cold, hardwood floor.

The knocking stopped and was replaced by an evil, hissing voice.

"Get out!"

I rushed out of the house, to my car and spent the night in a hotel. The next day I put the house on the market and told my real estate agent to sell it as fast as she could. Against her advice, I took the first offer I got. I just wanted to get rid of it.

I took an approximate fifteen thousand dollar loss.

I moved out on September 30th.

THE OCTOBER 13th HOUSE
The Other Bidder

The house was perfect. It was everything my wife and I wanted. A nice peaceful neighborhood. A back porch that overlooked a beautiful pond and a well-respected school district for when we were ready to start a family.

We put in a bid slightly over the asking price. We assumed we would get it with no problem, but apparently there was another person who wanted the house just as badly as we did and a bidding war ensued.

It took every penny we had saved to issue our initial bid so we weren't able to hang with the other bidder for long and lost the house.

I was upset, but my wife was devastated. She so had her heart set on that house that she went into a depression.

Oh, we kept looking for another house and we found some we liked, but for my wife, none of them stacked up to the house she had fallen in love with and she refused to settle for anything less.

I hated seeing her like that. She had dealt with depression most of her life and had been doing well the past few years, but losing the house really seemed to drive her over the edge. When she attempted suicide by taking a handful of pills, I guess I lost my mind a little bit.

I started parking outside our dream home and began watching the woman who outbid us. Her name was on the mailbox and it wasn't difficult to track her down on social media, which she was very active on.

Interestingly enough, it turned out that the reason she sold her previous house was because she thought it was haunted.

I work in the movie industry and had access to oodles of special effects. So, one day, after the woman went to work, I broke into the house, pulled up one of the flooring planks in the living room and inserted a small audio device. There were a myriad of sounds I could play through the device. Ultimately I decided upon a knocking sound.

As long as I was parked within two hundred feet of the house, I could activate the device at will. At first I played it just once in a while and I monitored her social media pages. Once it seemed like she was concerned, I gradually ramped up the frequency of the knocking.

It was late on a very stormy night when I decided to raise the stakes. I parked down the street, snuck up to the house, hid in the bushes and observed the living room through the window as I activated the knocking. It didn't take long for her to come downstairs. She was white as a ghost. When I spoke the words "get out" into the audio device, I feared for a few seconds that the poor woman may have a heart attack. Instead, she simply fled the premises. Once she was gone, I retrieved the recording device from the floor and hoped for the best.

The next day she put the house up for sale. I put in a lowball offer and it was instantly accepted. Everything went extremely smooth and fast.

We moved into the house on October 12th.

THE END

Chunks of Terror Vol. 3
Coming Soon

FINAL WORD

"Hudgins is a Horror-Meister to reckon with!"
VICTOR MILLER – *Writer of Friday the 13th*

Did you enjoy *Chunks of Terror Vol. 2?*
I hope so. And if you want more, which I'm sure you do, you won't have to wait long.
Volume 3 which will be available soon. Very soon.

While you wait, if you haven't read my other horror anthology series yet, I think you should!

FRAGMENTS OF FRIGHT

If you haven't read this international bestselling series yet, you're in for a terrifying treat!
You can grab the entire *Fragments of Fright* collection at the link below. All 5 Volumes bundled together into one huge boxed set!
https://www.amazon.com/dp/B0CM1GGVRR

Or if you prefer to go volume to volume, you can find all of them here:
https://www.amazon.com/dp/B0C3Z1RB7J

BLOOD TINGLING TALES

Blood Tingling Tales is another international best seller and is one of my most popular books.

You can get the entire Blo*od Tingling Tales* collection at the link below. All 5 volumes bundled together into one convenient boxed set!

https://www.amazon.com/gp/product/B0BWVJZB2T

Or if you prefer to go volume to volume, you can find all of them here:

https://www.amazon.com/dp/B0BK43LJNF

HORROR QUICKIES

Before *Chunks of Terror, Fragments of Fright* and *Blood Tingling Tales* there was *Horror Quickies*! The entire collection of 5 volumes can be found at the following link:

https://www.amazon.com/dp/B0BC4WTPD6

Or if you prefer to read one volume at a time, you can find all the individual volumes here:

https://www.amazon.com/dp/B09WK689P8

FROM THE MIND OF A MANIAC

I can't leave without letting everyone know about this bargain!

I bundled all 8 of my stand alone books into one gigantic boxed set. All 8 stories are interconnected in some way.

You get 8 books for the price of 1! The value is off the charts!

You can get *From the Mind of a Maniac* here:

https://www.amazon.com/dp/B0BZLXJ9R8

ACKNOWLEDGEMENTS

Thanks so much to my creepy yet wonderful advanced reader team A.K.A. *The Super Maniacs!*
Also big thanks to Doreen and Sherie for helping me in the endless battle against typos!
Cheers go out to Naomi for her terrifyingly awesome cover work!
And of course a huge thank you to every one of my maniacal fans out there in the world, wherever you are!

WHERE TO FIND ME

To keep up on my latest books you can visit my Amazon Author Page where all of my books are listed by popularity:
https://www.amazon.com/stores/Steve-Hudgins/author/B07KH2GMBF

Or you can visit the book section of my website which will show a list of my books from newest to oldest:
https://www.maniacontheloose.com/books

You can find all the audiobooks I have available here:
https://www.maniacontheloose.com/audiobooks

While you're at my website, be sure to sign up for my newsletter. You'll get access to some free stuff and be kept up to date on all the latest crazy things I have going on! Or sign up now:
https://subscribepage.io/maniac

At my website you may notice a PODCAST button. There you will find my podcast, *Maniac on the Loose Scary Stories*. It's where I read some of my short horror stories accompanied by creepy background music! I release new episodes every week.
Here's the link to that:
https://www.maniacontheloose.com/podcasts

Another section of my website that you may spot is the MOVIES section.
At one time I was making no-budget feature length indie horror films. If you want to check any of those out you can just follow this link to find out what streaming outlets they are available on, but keep in mind these were all made with no budget and it shows:
https://www.maniacontheloose.com/bigbiting pigproductions

If you want to follow me on any social media places this is where you can find me!

Goodreads:
https://www.goodreads.com/author/show/186
24636.Steve_Hudgins
Bookbub:
https://www.bookbub.com/profile/steve-
hudgins
Facebook:
https://www.facebook.com/SteveHudginsWri
ter
Twitter/X:
https://twitter.com/BigBitingPig

I hope *Chunks of Terror Vol. 2* terrified you in a
sick, fun kind of a way.
More is coming very soon!

www.maniacontheloose.com

Made in the USA
Columbia, SC
08 September 2024

41871607R00138